UNDER THE MOON

DEBORAH KERBEL

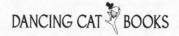
DANCING CAT BOOKS

The publisher gratefully acknowledges the support of the Canada Council for the Arts
and the Ontario Arts Council for its publishing program. We acknowledge the
financial support of the Government of Canada through the Canada Book Fund (CBF)
for our publishing activities, and the Government of Ontario through the
Ontario Media Development Corporation, an agency of the Ontario Ministry of
Culture, and the Ontario Book Publishing Tax Credit Program.

LIBRARY AND ARCHIVES CANADA CATALOGUING IN PUBLICATION

Kerbel, Deborah
Under the moon / Deborah Kerbel.

Issued also in electronic formats.
ISBN 978-1-77086-090-2

1. Title.

PS8621.E75U64 2012   JC813'.6   C2012-900275-5

Cover art and design: Angel Guerra/Archetype
Interior text design: Tannice Goddard, Soul Oasis Networking

Printer: Trigraphik LBF

Printed and bound in Canada.

The inside pages of this book are printed on 100% post-consumer waste recycled paper.

DANCING CAT BOOKS
An imprint of Cormorant Books Inc.
390 Steelcase Road East, Markham, Ontario, L3R 1G2
www.dancingcatbooks.com • www.cormorantbooks.com

For Kim
With love.

PROLOGUE

June 12th

The school bus chugs up the long, sloping driveway. Excited teen-age chatter bounces around me like a Super Ball. I sit by myself in the next-to-last row, head down, hands pushing into my pockets, holding my breath until my lungs start to singe and wishing this rickety old bus would succumb to a sudden death. Harsh, I know, but at least it would spare me the pain of what's coming. When we finally reach the top, I lift my head slightly and let the burning breath out. The old wooden cabin rolls into sight. There's no sign of anyone.

Quel relief.

She must still be inside.

I pull a hand out of my pocket and wipe away the film of sweat that's beading my upper lip. My armpits are feeling sweaty too. I'm melting with nerves. Normally, Aunt Su's shambly little cabin is my favourite place in the world. But on this sunny June day, I'm wishing I could be anywhere else on the planet. Solitary confine-ment in a dank, dungeonous, rodent-infested Columbian prison cell would be preferable.

Truly.

The bus wheezes to a stop and kids scramble into the aisles, eager to see the home of Big Bend's one and only author. Yeah, my Aunt Su holds a bit of a freak-show status around these parts (which I'm sure must thrill her to no end). I guess writers are rare in hayseed towns like ours, kind of like tropical birds over the Nunavut tundra.

Last year, in the hopes of "inspiring a new generation of budding artists," my teacher, Ms. Harris, asked me to arrange this class visit to Aunt Su's home. After months of nagging, I finally set it up. Now that the day is here, I'm praying with every cell in my body that artists are the only things my teacher will find budding around the old cabin.

"We're here, everybody out!" hollers our bus driver, a middle-aged man with a sagging pot-belly and a pair of matching dragon tattoos breathing fire out of each forearm. It's a warm spring afternoon but that doesn't stop a cool shiver of nerves from crawling over my skin as I imagine every cringe-worthy moment that might possibly take place in the next hour. Trust me, if you could peek into my brain right now, you wouldn't blame me for being the last one out of my seat. By the time I gather the nerve to get my legs moving, our driver is already ambling down to the edge of the property for a cigarette. I shuffle my way out of the bus. I'm definitely not in any kind of a hurry to get the visit started. Believe you me. Don't misunderstand; I love my Aunt Su like *whoa*. But other people just don't get her like I do.

Outside, Ms. Harris huddles us together in the driveway like a flock of unruly sheep. "Class, please wait here a moment while I check to make sure Ms. Chase is ready for us." She walks up the flagstone path toward the cabin. The second she's gone, every eye in the group turns to yours truly. Questions fly at me like a swarm of hungry black flies.

"*This* is where your aunt lives?"

"I thought authors were rich."

"Isn't she worried the walls are going to fall down?"

"How can she stand living all the way out here on her own?"

"My dad says your aunt is nuts."

It feels like there's a small animal chewing its way through my stomach. *Merde.* Why didn't I just play sick and stay in bed this morning? I duck my head away from the questions, close my eyes, and pretend to be invisible. A minute later, Ms. Harris is back. "Okay, people, she's ready for us. We can go in."

And suddenly, the small animal inside me is spinning around and crunching down on my spleen. I stagger forward through the pain. As my classmates file through the front door of the cabin, I send out a desperate series of silent, last-ditch prayers to the universe.

Please let her have some clothes on ... please don't let her be smoking anything ... please don't let me die of mortification ...

Aunt Su is waiting for us in her living room. She's dressed (*thank you, universe!*) in a flowing, lavender-coloured muumuu that trails behind her like some kind of elegant ball gown. She's wearing her best faux feather earrings, and her long grey hair has been pulled up into a high, swingy ponytail. She grins widely and winks as soon as she spots me. Then she lifts her arms over her head and starts waving her hands frantically to beckon the rest of the kids closer. The room is cluttered with all her crazy stuff, so we all just stand in a wobbly circle and listen while she speaks. She talks for a few minutes about writing and passion and emotions. She shows us her overflowing bookcases and tells us about her love of reading. "Remember kids, every writer is a reader first." It's her favourite saying; I must have heard it a thousand times over the years. Then she plucks a dog-eared novel off the shelf and reads a passage out loud to us. It's a really sad passage, and she injects her heart into each word. By the end, she has half of us entranced and the other half in tears. Me, I'm somewhere in between.

Before we can recover, she flips on some Mozart and shoos everybody over to the giant picture window that faces the lake. The sun is shining on the waves, and it sparkles like a field of diamonds as the notes of the symphony fill the room. One by one, we take turns describing to her what we see in the water. After that, she hands out pens and sheets of paper and leads us through a writing exercise. There's nowhere in the cabin for twenty-one kids to sit and write, so Aunt Su has us stand in a big circle and lean forward so that our backs become desks for the person behind us. We bend our bodies and write through the hilariously ticklish pen scratches across our spines. By the time we're done, the entire room is belly-laughing, even stone-faced Ms. Harris. With so many warm, happy bodies, the little cabin is quickly transforming into a makeshift sauna, and there isn't a drop of air conditioning around for kilometres. Aunt Su skips over to her freezer, pulls out a giant box of grape-flavoured Popsicles, and ushers us out onto the lakefront porch for a snack. Ms. Harris suddenly turns stone-faced again.

"Excuse me, Ms. Chase, but are those peanut-free? Our school has a strict policy …"

Aunt Su snorts and passes the Popsicle box around the group. "Policy, schmolicy. It's just frozen water! You're in my home now, not school."

Ms. Harris doesn't even try to argue with that one.

The group volume lowers while we all suck on the Popsicles and enjoy the cool breeze blowing off the lake. Aunt Su flits over to my side, her crinkly smile creasing her face like a beautiful Chinese fan. "How'd I do, my Lily-girl? Hope I didn't embarrass you too much."

I give her a big hug and notice how, under the muumuu, her body feels thinner than usual. "You were great," I say. And I mean it. She puts a hand on my cheek. Her palm is smooth and warm — like sunlight sliding over my skin. Her eyes narrow with worry. "You didn't sleep last night after our phone call, did you?"

I shake my head. "Too much on my mind." I don't tell her the rest of the truth — how worrying about this class visit kept my brain from getting any rest. Seems silly, now that it went so well.

Pirouetting around, she extracts a book from a small cardboard box on the porch floor and hands it to me.

"My newest baby arrived in the mail this morning. Want to see?"

Nodding, I turn the book over in my hands and examine the glossy cover. A beautiful young couple is embracing in a swirling ocean as a dark, ominous sky looms above. The title reads *LoveStorm*.

"If you ask me, the font they used is all wrong," she says, pointing at her pen name streaking across the cover in thick, black Times New Roman letters. "Not my personality at all. But I do like the picture they came up with. What do you think?"

"Except for the font, I like it. A lot." If people were fonts, Aunt Su would definitely be ◆)(■Ŋ♌♑)(■Ŋ♌◆. (That's wingdings, in case you don't know enough about fonts to tell.) I hand the book back to her with a sigh that says, *Just wish I could read it for myself.*

I might as well have screamed the words out loud, because Aunt Su can see my thoughts as clearly as if my forehead was made of glass. She smiles sadly and tweaks my chin. "That's something you have to take up with your mother, Lily-girl."

My mother. Just the mention of her makes me squirm in my flip-flops.

As I'm bending down to put *LoveStorm* back in the box, Emma Swartz and her Siamese-twin-BFF Sarah Rein come up to me. "Your aunt's really cool!" they swoon in unison. "How often do you come here? This cabin seems like such a great place to

hang out." These two girls never talk to me at school. Like, ever.
So I'm guessing they must be genuinely impressed by Aunt Su.
The little animal has long since stopped chewing on my stomach.
Now there's something else inside me … something warm and
light filling my chest like a helium balloon. I think it might just be
happiness. Or maybe pride. Or maybe both.

The visit is over. While Ms. Harris stays back to thank Aunt
Su, the rest of us follow the narrow path up the side of the cabin
to get back to the bus. I'm so chuffed about the way the afternoon
went, I must stop thinking clearly. Because next thing I know, I'm
leading the group right past Aunt Su's herb garden. That's when
it happens. Todd Nelson breaks away from the path and kneels
down in the garden, turning one of the tiny new spring plants
over in his hands. My heart freezes the second I realize what he's
found. Todd's family is in the gardening business. He happens to
know more about plants than any other kid in Big Bend. "Oh my
God," he calls out to us. "She's growing marijuana!"

Waves of shocked laughter slam into me from all sides, and in
a flash of a second, I feel that happy little helium balloon burst
apart inside me. My cheeks flare with an angry heat. *Don't laugh
at my aunt,* I want to yell at them. But I don't. Instead, I tear away
from the group, back to the bus, back to my seat in the next-to-
last row, where I bury my face in the green vinyl bench, close my
eyes, and pretend to be invisible. Again.

A Short Note from Me

You probably never thought of this before, so I guess it's kind of my duty to enlighten you to the reality of the situation. Are you ready? It's sort of depressing — maybe you should be sitting down. Because the sad fact is that while you're sleeping every night — snoring and pillow drooling and twisting like a giant piece of licorice under the sheets — a huge chunk of life passes you by. Truly. By the time you're old and shrivelled up, you'll have slept away 220,000 hours, or about 9,125 days. That's almost twenty-five years gone in the blink of a dream.

Twenty-five years!

I'll give you a couple of seconds to process that.

A Short Note from Me (Part 2)

Okay, that's enough. Now that you've had some time to absorb, you're probably starting to wonder what you'd do with all that extra time you'd have if you didn't have to sleep. Am I right?

Well, you've come to the right place, my friend. I can tell you the answer to that question 'cause I happen to be the only person in the world who's alive to write about it. Yes, the *only* person in the world (and if you don't believe me, just watch for my name in the upcoming edition of *Guinness World Records*). If you didn't have to sleep, you'd get to know the dark really well. Trust me on this one. And you'd come up with some creative ways to pass the time to keep yourself from going mental — like writing a novel or re-enacting the Defenestration of Prague. And you'd rack your brains for something amazing to do. And you'd become friends with the moon and pretty much anything and everything else that comes out at night.

At least, that's what I'm doing.

It all started with a dead body.

My Aunt Su's, to be specific …

ONE

A pair of scuffed black loafers creak across the wooden floor and slow to a stop in front of me. Sturdy, practical, and straight out of the Librarians "R" Us catalogue. I know without looking up that they belong to one of the bazillion old ladies who've descended on my house today — all claiming to be old friends of my Aunt Su's.

"Are you all right, dear?" a soft, grey voice asks from above. A sudden image of afternoon tea, lace doilies, and raspberry scones fills my head. I nod and keep my eyes on the floor. The voice is nice enough, but I know if I say a word, I'll start to cry. And once I start, I might never be able to stop again.

Ever.

"We're all so sorry about your aunt. Such a shock."

My hands instinctively curl into fists at my sides. If one more person tells me how sorry they are, I'm going to have to start throwing some punches. A fistfight at a funeral reception — Aunt Su would have loved that. Hockey was the only thing she ever watched on her fuzzy old TV, and I happen to know she only enjoyed it for the blood. I glance sideways at the small, pomegranate-shaped jar perched on the mantle. The sight of it sends my stomach plunging into my socks.

After a moment, the loafers give up and retreat back to the

herd of sensible shoes that are whispering and shuffling around the dining room table. My shoulders sag with relief as I watch them go. I don't want to share stories and tears with any of Aunt Su's childhood friends. I don't want them telling me how sorry they are and hugging me to their thick, perfumy chests. I don't want any of these strangers to see how broken I am inside. All I want is for this day to be over so I can have my house back and grieve alone.

A trickle of sweat dribbles a path down my back. With all these extra bodies crowded into our house, the air is unbearably hot and stuffy. I fan myself with my hands as the old ladies' hushed words blow across my ears like a slow breeze.

"... so sudden ... accidental overdose ... how much do you think ... such a strange little niece ..."

I squeeze my eyes shut and will away the sudden rush of tears that's threatening to burst out and tear me to pieces. When I open them again, there's another pair of shoes parked in front of me. I know right away these shoes won't be so easy to get rid of. Black patent leather, sharp three-inch heels, and one pointy toe tapping the floor with obvious impatience.

My mother.

"Lily?"

I keep my eyes on the floor and pretend not to hear. *Lily.* I still don't know what possessed my parents to name me after a flower. A girl named Lily should be sweet and delicate with a voice that rings like a bell — dontcha think? Pretty much the opposite of me. I have nothing even remotely delicate going on (unless you count my puny height, which my mother insists on calling "petite") and my voice is more of a gong than a bell. I know it's technically wrong, but I like to think of myself as an oxymoron.

And no, that's not a brand of zit cream.

"You haven't eaten a thing today, Lily. You'll make yourself sick if you're not careful."

"I'm not hungry," I manage to say without imploding.

"Honey, you're not the only one hurting here, you know. We miss her too."

No you don't. Not like I do.

A soggy-looking tuna fish sandwich suddenly appears in front of my face.

"I brought this for you. Eat. It'll help."

My eyes flick up to Mom for a second. Her forehead is scrunched up like an accordion and her blue eyes are all dark and squinty. She actually looks worried.

"Eat," she says again, pushing the sandwich so close it almost squishes my nose.

Brilliant, Mom — like some goopy canned fish and day-old bread will solve all my problems. I know my mother means well, but whatever maternal instincts allowed her to give birth to me have long since gone on a permanent leave of absence. Shoving some smelly fish into my face is the best she can muster up in the way of comfort. I shouldn't be surprised; when I was little, instead of kissing my cuts and bruises like the other mothers did, my mom used to tell me to toughen up and shake off the pain. Epic mom-fail, right?

But even though she's clueless and sad, you kinda have to love her for trying. Mom is an accountant, but I honestly believe she missed her true calling by not pursuing a career in the military — she would have made an A1 army officer. Sometimes I call her General MacArthur in my head.

"Eat," she commands in that certain tone that tells me I'm out of options.

"Okay, fine." I accept the sandwich and take a small bite, because I know she'll never leave me alone if I don't. For every second I chew, the black pointy toe taps a bit slower. After another bite of the sandwich, I hear a loud sigh, and then my mother's shoes turn and clack away towards the kitchen. As soon as they're out of sight, I drop the sandwich onto the empty couch cushion beside me, close my eyes, and wish for the millionth time that Aunt Su was here to get me through this heinous day.

I mean, how messed up is that? I'm actually wishing for my dead aunt to come and help me get through her own funeral reception. But she's truly the only person who could do it. The only person who's ever been able to make me feel better on the absolute worst days. And today definitely is a gold-medal contender for the worst of the absolute worst!

When I open my eyes again, I see that a couple of familiar size thirteen runners have planted themselves in front of me. In Dad's hurry to get to the funeral on time, his left pant leg's been tucked deeply into his fashion-deviant white gym sock.

Mom must have been supremely distracted not to have noticed that unforgiveable breach of funerary dress code. For about the millionth time, I wonder how my parents ended up marrying each other. Seriously, the only thing those two have in common is me. It's probably a good thing they divorced before I was old enough to talk. Just the thought of them living in the same house together makes me want to slam my head against a brick wall. At least they're decent to each other at times like this when they're forced to co-parent.

"I can tell your mother's worried about you," Dad says. "She only pushes food into your mouth when she's freaking out."

I swallow the hard lump that's rising in my throat and battle to keep my voice from leaking into a whine.

"Whatever, Dad."

"But if you don't get that sandwich off the couch PDQ, I'm going to start worrying too. She'll make you do push-ups if there's a stain."

Tragically, he isn't joking. I pick the sandwich up and hand it to him.

"Here. I'm not hungry."

Dad inhales the remains of my sandwich and plops himself down on the couch beside me. I can tell he's distracted because he doesn't even stop to pull the trusty little bottle of Tabasco sauce out of his pocket. He leans forward, elbows on his lap as his blue eyes scramble to catch mine. "Come on, Sweetness — it's going to be okay."

I shake my head hard, refusing to look at him. "No, it's not."

"Yes, it will. You'll see. The sun will shine again. Just give it time."

I feel his strong arm wrap around my shoulders and pull me into a tight hug. "We'll get through this together, Lil."

Yeah, this sorry little pep talk is the best my dad's going to be able to do. And as you've probably already guessed, it isn't nearly enough to help. I mean, for Pete's sake — the only person on the planet who's ever loved me has been reduced to a tropical fruit–shaped jarful of ashes and he's talking about sunshine?

Okay, before you get the wrong idea, yeah, I know my parents love me — but they kind of *have* to love me because they're my parents. It's not like they ever had much of a choice. And honestly, I don't always get the impression that they like me all that much. Not that I blame them, mind you. I can admit it: I'm not always the easiest kid in the world to like. But Aunt Su was different. She loved me and liked me and knew me and heard me and *got* me. If you're ever lucky enough to have someone like that in your life, never let them go. Trust me on this one. Chances are you won't ever find a person like that again.

"So any idea who invited the sewing circle?" Dad asks, nodding toward the convention of black-clad denture models still hovering in the dining room.

"I think they're old friends of Aunt Su's."

Dad snorts. "They don't exactly look like the type of people Su would choose to hang out with."

I shrug. What can I say? He's right. Aunt Su was my mother's much, *much* older half-sister. She was twenty-four years old and already graduated from university when Mom was born — they'd never even lived in the same house. But even though Aunt Su was technically old enough to be my grandmother, she was one of those adults who never really grew up. She lived alone in that shambly old cabin by the lake, where she wrote all day and churned out trashy romance novels by the dozens. I've always wanted to read one, but Mom says they're pretty racy and won't let me until I'm sixteen (which is only five months away, so I don't know what the big deal is). Aunt Su was the kind of person old people like to call "eccentric." Unpredictable, unreadable, and, well, wingdingish. She dressed exclusively in purple and green (when she bothered getting dressed at all), only dated men who were half her age, drove a moped around town from spring to fall, and smoked pot daily to help battle writer's block. And she would drop everything and come running any time I needed her. She loved me like a best friend, sister, mother, and aunt all rolled into one big hug that never ended. She was the world to me. Since she died, the days have lost their shape. But the nights are so much worse.

Leaning forward, I peer out the living room window into the blackening sky. There isn't going to be a moon tonight. I know this for a fact.

Releasing my shoulder, Dad lets out a tired sigh and tilts his head back to rest on the couch pillows. His hairy hands come together to cover his face like a small, dark tent. "God, I don't know why funerals always wipe me out. Tonight of all nights, I could really use a good sleep. When do you think this crowd is going to take the hint and leave already? I want to go home."

Sleep.

Just the thought of it brings a gross wave of panic crashing through my stomach. Counting the red seconds flicker by one at a time as the hours stretch in front of me like kilometres of empty grey highway.

"I don't know, Dad. Hopefully they'll leave soon."

"How've you been sleeping lately, Sweetness?"

"Um, fine," I lie. "About three or four hours a night."

"Okay, that's good," Dad replies. He doesn't even look up. That's because three or four hours of sleep sounds halfway human, which is pretty much all he wants to hear. If adults think everything is going okay, they leave you alone. All most parents want are kids that are semi-normal.

Not nocturnal mutants like me.

I stare back up at the pomegranate jar and let out a long, slow breath.

Aunt Su is gone forever.

Merde!

How the hell am I ever going to get through the nights without her?

TWO

I was right about the moon. It was like the sky was dipped in ink last night. Even the stars couldn't manage to power through the thick cover of cloud that coated the sky. It was the kind of night that was made of sinister. The kind of night that could swipe a person's hope. I stared out my window until the sun came up, watching the darkness, afraid to turn my back on it for a second. And then this morning, the sun came out and burned away all the clouds. Which meant the moon would be back tonight. Which made me feel good. I knew it couldn't stay hidden forever.

Tap, tap, tap.

Mom's shoe is at it again. Beating against the marble floor of Mr. Duffy's office in a frenzied display of hyper. Reaching out, I put a hand on her knee to stop the racket but she just starts tapping the other foot instead. With a sigh, I glance up at the clock, still not entirely sure why Aunt Su's lawyer invited us to meet with him today. Dad said it's just a routine kind of process after someone dies — estate settlement or something. I guess I'm about to find out exactly what that means. If Dad ever gets here, that is. He's already twenty minutes late for the meeting — hardly a big surprise. I don't know why Mom isn't used to it by now; it's not like he's ever been on time even once in his life. My grandpa always likes to joke about how lateness is embedded into the family genes. "Our ancestors sailed over to America on the *Juneflower*, you know, shrimp?"

Now that I think about it, it's probably one of the main reasons my parents divorced.

The little bald lawyer checks his watch, clears his throat softly, and shuffles through the stack of papers on his desk. That stack of papers is Aunt Su's will — her last words to us and the only reason we're gathered in this pretentious office wallpapered with legal degrees and awards.

An image of my aunt's crinkly face floats in front of my eyes, bringing on that all-too-familiar sting of tears. At sixty-two years old and after a lifetime of laughing, the skin on Aunt Su's face had been sculpted into a permanent smile. Just thinking of her dead makes me feel so empty — like I could easily dissolve away into nothing. The sting in my eyes is starting to grow into a burn, but the last thing I want to do is cry here in front of Mom and this odd-looking little lawyer. When I cry, I like to be alone. Squeezing my lids shut to keep the tears away, I cross my arms in front of my chest and wish for the millionth time that my aunt was still alive. The past few nights have been a waking nightmare without her. And with no moon for company, last night was the worst.

Let me be clear on this: I've never been much of a sleeper, even before Aunt Su died. My body's just not wired for it. I wouldn't call it insomnia, exactly — I'm just one of those people who don't need as much sleep as others. When I was a baby, I would stay awake for twenty hours out of every day. Mom says she wanted to throw me out the window back then.

I like to give her the benefit of the doubt and assume that's a joke.

And as I got older, my sleeping just got worse. When I was a toddler, I'd stay up most of the night banging on the crib rails and screaming for someone to come play with me. After I outgrew my crib, Mom says she had to lock my bedroom door every night to keep me from wandering around and getting into trouble (and from barging into her room and waking her up). By that point, I'd exhausted her to the point of desperation. Guess I can't exactly blame her or Dad for never wanting to have any more kids.

As soon as I was old enough to figure out how to dial a telephone, I started calling Aunt Su to talk. No matter how late it was, she was always happy to hear from me. She'd spend hours with me on the phone, helping me pass the time until I could fall asleep for a little bit. Now that I'm a teenager, I sleep less than ever. Until lately, one or two hours seemed to be all I needed. But Aunt Su was always there to help me get through the nights. Then she died, and everything about my life flipped upside down. Nobody else knows this, but in the nine days since she's been gone the sickest thing has happened. I haven't been able to sleep at all. Seriously, like not even a minute. And the really weird part is that I'm not even tired. How whacked is that?

Beside me, Mom sighs loudly, crosses her legs, and starts drumming the other toe against the floor. She's getting more wound up with every second Dad makes us wait. Poor guy is going to get slapped with such a bitch-face when he finally gets here. Have I mentioned that my mother is a major control freak? Always has been. And it's getting worse lately. Yeah, it's so bad, she can't even give up control long enough to follow a cookbook recipe. I've actually seen her get angry at a box of cake mix for trying to tell her what to do.

S'truth.

If people were fonts, my mother would be CASTELLAR. Stiff, standing-to-attention, all-caps. A font to be reckoned with. She *really* doesn't cope well with people who don't follow the rules (which, I'm sure, is the main reason why she never got along with

Aunt Su). So, imagine her reaction if she knew that my body's decided to stop sleeping altogether. She'd completely and totally freak out. Which is exactly why I haven't said anything about this to either of my parents. Coping on my own is just better. Believe you me.

Suddenly, there's a knock at the door. I whirl around in my seat to see Dad's smiling face poking into the room. "Hey. Sorry I'm late. Did I miss anything?"

Mom's hands clench the armrests of her chair so hard, her knuckles turn white. "For God's sake, Ro, just come in and sit down," she hisses.

With a rush of warm air, Dad plops himself down in the empty seat beside me, smelling faintly of the large coffee and chocolate doughnut I know he must have eaten for lunch on the way over. Crumbs on his chin and stains on his shirt always reveal the complete menu selections of his last meal. Along with, of course, the layer of permanent Tabasco sauce drips on his tie. Dad always brings a little bottle of that spicy stuff to every meal, and he dribbles it on everything he eats. He's half Sri Lankan, which means he loves spicy things. Why he chose my mother, I'll never understand. Yet another good example of how my parents were so totally and completely mismatched from the get-go.

I cover Dad's hand with mine to let him know I'm not mad at him for being late. But I won't be able to save him from Mom's temper — he'll have to deal with that on his own. Right now she's glowering at him over my head. I can practically feel the buzz of irritation radiating off her skin.

"Look what the cat dragged in," she says, her voice like sandpaper.

He winks at her and smiles in reply, incredibly unfazed by her ferocious inner beast. I slouch down in my seat and pray for the lawyer to get this thing started. Almost like he can read my mind,

Mr. Duffy folds his stubby, manicured fingers in into a neat little ball and nods at us.

"Okay, thank you all for coming. We're here today to settle the estate of Susan Marie Chase. It's quite a simple, straightforward document and won't take very long to review."

Mom holds up a hot-pink manicured finger. "Beet It" is her signature nail polish colour — she's worn it every day since the beginning of time. We should have bought stock. "Excuse me, Mr. Duffy, but if the document is so straightforward, why are we here?" she asks. "Couldn't you just have mailed copies out to us?"

Mr. Duffy clears his throat, his voice rising up high into a funny little squeak. "Yes, well, normally I don't invite an audience to this kind of thing. But, as you know, your sister had, I guess you could politely call it, a 'flair for the dramatic.' She specifically asked that I conduct a personal will reading. And in this case, it's not a bad idea. I'm anticipating that there might be some … concerns." He shuffles the papers in front of him. I can tell he's avoiding Mom's gaze. "Before we get started, are there any questions?"

Dad waves a meaty hand in the air, just like an oversized schoolkid. "Sorry Mr. Duffy, but are we *it*? Isn't there anybody else coming to this thing?"

The lawyer shakes his head. "No one else has been invited. You three are the only people whose presence is required at the meeting here today. Any other questions?"

Three heads shake simultaneously.

"Fine. Shall we begin, then?"

Without even waiting for our answer, he pops on a pair of large, black-rimmed glasses, picks up the sheet of paper at the top of the pile, and begins reading aloud.

"This document was last updated in June of this year and states: 'I, Susan Marie Chase being of sound mind …'"

Mr. Duffy looks up from the paper and peers at us over the rims of his glasses. "Forgive me, but my client has explicitly instructed me to insert the words 'har-har' at this point in the document."

I can practically hear the scream Mom is forcing herself to hold back. Out of the corner of my eye, I see Dad's shoulders quake as he clamps a hand over his mouth to hide the laughter. With a slight shake of his head, Mr. Duffy continues.

"'... do hereby declare this instrument to be my last will and testament. I hereby revoke all previous wills and codicils. Now let's get on with it. To my sister, Lisa MacArthur, I hereby bequeath a long-overdue sense of humour and the everlasting hope that she will finally lighten up and begin to allow space for some joy into her rigid world.'"

I suck in a nervous breath. Glancing over at Mom, I see that her face is turning a disturbingly deep shade of red. Bullets shoot out of her blue eyes and fly across the room at the lawyer's head. Mr. Duffy ducks slightly and keeps reading Aunt Su's crazy will (even though the expression on his face makes it seem like a giant pin is sticking into his butt).

"'To my brother-in-law, Roshan MacArthur, I hereby bequeath a cheque for ten thousand dollars to be donated to his charity and an eternity of gratitude for raising the world's most wonderful kid.'"

Dad takes my hand and gives it a proud squeeze while Mr. Duffy pauses to adjust his glasses.

"'And finally,'" he continues, "'I do hereby bequeath the remainder of my assets and worldly possessions to my niece, Lily MacArthur, along with the task of caring for and disposing of my remains. I appoint her father, Roshan MacArthur, to act as the executor of this will, to serve without bond. I herewith affix my signature to this will on this the twenty-ninth day of June, et cetera, et cetera.'"

And with that, Mr. Duffy drops the paper back onto the desk, closes his eyes, and pats down the increasingly shiny sides of his naked pink head.

Bequeath. Funny word. It sounds like a lispy Shakespearian curse. *A bequeathing pestilence upon thee!*

For a few seconds it's so quiet in that room, I can hear the air from the ceiling fan swirling around my ears. *Um, okay, is that it?*

"So does that mean what I think it means?" I finally manage to say, glancing over at my mother for an explanation. She doesn't notice me because her eyes are cemented to Mr. Duffy's pinched face.

"Excuse me, are you saying that, except for ten thousand dollars, the entirety of the estate goes to Lily?" Her words are heavy and thick, like a slab of solid granite.

"Yes, that's what the document says," he says, pointing at the paper. "It's really quite clear. Indisputable, actually. Here, have a look."

Mom grabs the paper from him and slides her eyes down the page. "But this makes no sense. She's only a child. What on earth will she do with it?"

Mr. Duffy pulls off his glasses and places them carefully down onto his desk.

"Mrs. MacArthur, I assure you that the appropriate provisions have been put in place. The assets are to be held in trust until your daughter reaches the age of majority."

Age of majority? Remainder of assets? Disposal of remains? I rise to my feet slowly, praying my wobbly knees will keep me up. "Um, hello? Can you guys please stop talking about me as if I'm not here and tell me what's going on?"

Dad reaches for my hand and pulls me back down into my chair. "Sweetness, it means that you're pretty much Aunt Su's sole heir. She's left all her stuff to you. Including her ashes."

My pulse is starting to throb in my ears. Aunt Su left everything she had to *me*?

Before I can say another word, Mom's on her feet, one hand on her bony hip and the other wagging a long, beet-coloured fingernail at the lawyer. "This is insanity! Did you have a hand in drafting this document? Su has always been a questionable influence on a young, impressionable girl. How could she possibly have thought this was a good idea? What does a fifteen-year-old need with a rundown cabin, a stash of marijuana, and a stack of smutty books?"

"Calm down now, Lisa," Dad says. "Mr. Duffy here is just following Su's instructions."

"Instructions? From a lunatic? Please! There should be a law against this kind of thing!"

Everything? Aunt Su left everything she had to me?

The room is suddenly unbearably small. Smaller than a darkroom. Smaller than a pomegranate jar. Smaller than a blink of a dream. Too small to do anything but drop my head into my hands and bite back another wave of tears while my parents fight over Aunt Su's last words.

As for me, I don't want any of her *bequeathing* stuff.

I just want my aunt back.

THREE

Fact #1: The stucco ceiling in my bedroom has nineteen thousand, seven hundred and fifty-two tiny bumps of paint sticking out of it.

Fact #2: Only a pathologically bored individual would know something like this.

Fact #3: Lately, I absolutely hate being me.

Sorry, did I mention that last one already?

With a sigh verging on a scream, I flip my pillow over onto the cool side and stare out my open window. The night breeze blowing on my face smells sweet — like dying roses and wet grass. A pale sliver of a new moon shines above a grey bank of clouds. So thin, it looks like a strong wind could snap it in half. It's just a hint of a moon — but it's enough. Like a tease of something bigger and better on the way.

I squeeze my eyes shut, bringing swirls of colours and shapes rising up behind my lids. And then I force myself to breathe really slowly, like people in movies do when they sleep.

Long breath in ... long breath out ... long breath in ... long breath out ...

But after a few minutes that just feels dumb. Flipping myself over the other way, I squeeze my eyes harder and conjure up a virtual barnyard of imaginary animals. Sheep, pigs, cows, horses ... you get the picture. And then I start counting. But by the time I hit a thousand, I know it's hopeless. *Sleep! Sleep now!* I silently command my body, doing a near-perfect impersonation of General MacArthur. But of course, my body, doing its best imitation of General MacArthur's stubborn daughter, doesn't listen.

Zut!

I must be the only person on the planet to have elaborate and recurring narcoleptic fantasies.

Damn it! What's wrong with me? Opening my eyes again, I roll over and snap on my bedside lamp.

3:09 a.m.

If you've ever been awake at this time, you would know that it's the ugliest, loneliest time on the clock. It always comes just after the moment when you feel like your brain is going to crack open from boredom. This is the time when all the most heinous parts of your life get replayed through your head in high def. The time when each and every moment of self-doubt is magnified through a super-power optical zoom lens. The time when loneliness starts to tip towards insanity and you begin to believe what you want most in the world is to fall asleep and never wake up again. This time of night is the absolute bottomless black hole of the clock.

But of course, you wouldn't know that, because you're normal enough to always sleep through it. Well, not me. As a nocturnal mutant, I get sucked straight into the black hole night after night after night.

In books and movies, it's pretty obvious that the only characters who don't sleep are freaks of nature like vampires or monsters, or superheroes who can only fight crime under the cover of darkness to keep their true identities a secret. Sometimes, to keep myself from tipping over that edge, I try to think of myself as a freak without a movie deal. It doesn't usually work. Lately, I've been wondering if it would help to reach out to other freaks of nature around the world and bond over our common crap-sucking plight. I mean, there *have* to be other sleepless freaks out there like me. I know about albinos and giants and hairy-faced people. But I've never heard of anyone else who doesn't need sleep. So I Googled it this afternoon after we got home from Mr. Duffy's office to find out a bit more, but that turned out to be a major mistake. Because guess what I learned?

Give up?

You're thinking that sleepless people turn into cranky, red-eyed Nyquil addicts, right? Not the worst kind of fate, comparatively speaking. But no, I learned from my Google search that human beings positively, inevitably, without exception *die* without sleep. In fact, from what I read on something called the National Sleep Research Project, it seems like the absolute longest anyone has ever gone without sleep has been eighteen days, twenty-one hours, and forty minutes.

Eighteen days!

Which pretty much explains why there are no other sleepless freaks like me to search out and bond with. They're all dead. And, apparently, pretty soon I will be too. I'm going on ten completely sleepless days now. So at this rate, I have just over a week left to save myself from an untimely demise.

I know what you're thinking: you're wondering why I don't just quit the complaining and take some Nyquil already. Right? Well, I tried that once. A few years back, Aunt Su took pity on me and sliced one of her sleeping pills in half and let me have it. But in the end, that little half pill didn't help me sleep. It just made me feel really jittery and sick.

Still, I know if Aunt Su were here, she could help me. She always did, you know. Well, except for the sleeping pill thing. I swear, she was the only person on the planet who could keep me from feeling like a Darwinian case study. She used to tell me that I was just an average, everyday, regular kid with a body that didn't like to follow the rules. "I've never been a fan of toeing the line myself, Lil," she used to say. "You're just taking after your aunt."

Man, I miss her. The pomegranate jar-of-death is sitting on my desk, awaiting its fate. According to Dad, I'm supposed to take some time and think of just the right place to scatter the ashes. Whatever that means. "You knew Su better than anyone else, Lily," he said on our way out of Mr. Duffy's office. "That's why she asked you to do it. Think of the things in life that made Aunt Su happy and then try to imagine where she'd want to spend the rest of her days."

Great, not much pressure there!

"But, Dad, what if I choose the wrong place?"

"There is no wrong place, Sweetness. Whatever you decide will be right."

"I don't get it," I moaned. "Why didn't she just tell me where she wanted to be scattered in the will?"

He just shrugged. "Guess she wanted you to figure it out for yourself."

Ugh. Don't you just hate it when old people talk like that? Suddenly, there's a panicky feeling of restlessness sneaking over my skin. I kick the sheet off my legs and pull myself out of bed. A soft breeze blows over my bare shoulders, sending an army of delicious goosebumps marching up my back. Overripe roses must be the sweetest smell the universe has ever produced. I'm telling you, if somebody could figure out how to bottle that smell, they could spray it through the air vents in office buildings and save tons of cash on corporate-sponsored anger management sessions. I breathe in a double lungful and hold it tightly inside, waiting for the calm to come over me. But I'm still feeling so wound up by what happened at the lawyer's office earlier this afternoon that not even the sweet summer night air can soothe away my stress. Aunt Su's last words have been running through my mind all day like the skipping chorus from a scratched up CD.

I do hereby bequeath the remainder of my worldly possessions to my niece ...

Worldly possessions. What on earth am I going to do with a closetful of funny clothes, a rusty moped, and a container of ashes? Of course, I'm interested in that collection of racy novels. Not being a total naïf, I think I have a pretty good idea of what I might find inside. But still, it would be cool to flip through the pages and see just what Mom's been keeping me away from all these years. Problem is that Mom has the only key to the cottage. And she's forbidden me from going over there until she's had a chance to sort through Aunt Su's stuff. I know she's none too thrilled about the kinds of things I've just inherited. And it probably doesn't help that those things all happen to be located next to the lake. Mom's always been nervous around water. She has this totally irrational fear of drowning. When she was little, she knew someone who drowned in the lake not too far from the Docks. Because of that one accident, she freaks out whenever I go anywhere near the water. I really think she'd make me wear a life preserver in the bathtub if she could. Truly. Just add it to the long list of reasons why she tries so hard to keep me away from Aunt Su's lakeside cabin.

Padding across the room, I sit down on the narrow ledge beneath my window. Outside, the silver moon is slicing its way through the dark sky. Like a random cut from a sharpened blade. I have a massive urge to go outside and get a better look at it, talk to it, ask it for directions.

Excuse me, sorry to bother, but I couldn't help noticing how perfect your view is from up there. You wouldn't happen to have seen any other Big Benders who're awake like me, would you?

All these sleepless nights are obviously starting to mess with my head. Yeah, I have to get out of here or I'm going to lose it completely. Normally, I do everything humanly possible to avoid the company of people. My social skills are embarrassingly deficient, and I always seem to say the wrong thing, no matter how hard I try. So usually I just don't try. But when the Reaper's knocking at your door, you get a little desperate. And truthfully, the idea of dying alone in my room is majorly depressing. My eyes flick over to the clock.

3:16.

I need to find someone else in this village who's awake like me. Or I'll go insane.

Oops, did I just say "village"? See what happened? You wrestled it out of me. Okay, so, technically we're a village, not a town. Big Benders don't like to fess up to that little fact, so don't tell them you heard it from me. They like to dream big around here. Especially the young ones. For most kids my age, this place is like Alcatraz: a remote prison they've been planning their escape from since the moment they could walk. Toronto, Montreal, Vancouver, New York — these cities are the ultimate goals. And if they could just make it across the frozen, shark-infested waters, they'd be free.

Me? I have no problem with village life. In fact, I kind of like it. The great thing about living in a village is that you have a lot of space. Everything's big. Big houses, big properties, big sky, big spaces, big dreams. The bad thing about living in a village is that not much happens in those big spaces and most everyone's big dreams eventually dry up and turn to dust. But since I'm probably the only teenager in this place who dreams of staying put, that last part isn't much of a problem for me.

It only takes me a couple of seconds to pull on a hoodie and a pair of sneakers. Jumping down from the second floor isn't nearly as hard as you'd think. There's a soft, thick patch of overgrown

grass right below my window that helps break my fall. Good thing
I haven't surrendered to my mother's command that I get off my
butt and mow the lawn before the neighbours start complaining.
Quel joke! As if any of our neighbours would care about a thing
like that. General MacArthur is the only one around here who
gives a rat's ass about having a manicured lawn.

It feels good to be outside. The air is warm and thick and damp
and soft on my skin — like walking through a bowl of mushroom
soup. I pull off my hoodie so I can let my bare arms soak up the
night air and scamper around the house up to the main road. Ever
take a walk by yourself at night? The sounds are totally different
than what you hear during the day. No traffic, no people, no birds
singing. Just night noises. I can hear the leaves swishing above me
in the trees. The crumply crunch of the gravel under my shoes —
like I'm walking across a big plate of cereal.

Grape-Nuts, I think.

Invisible crickets chirping from every direction. An owl hooting
from a nearby tree. The flap of wings over my head and then a
flurry of small, dark shapes against the darker sky.

Bats. *Awesome.*

I can't see much as I walk along the road, but to tell you the
truth I don't really have to. When you've walked the same road
every day for fifteen years, you commit every turn and bend to
memory. Believe you me. After about twenty minutes of walking,
I hear a rustling noise beside me. My heart pauses. A moment
later, a large, round raccoon ambles out in front of my path. Its
giant, glowing eyes find mine. I suck back a deep, calming breath
and wait for it to pass.

Just a raccoon, Lily. Don't get so scared over nothing!

As soon as my heart starts up again, I keep walking. There just
has to be somebody else awake. Doesn't there?

After a couple more kilometres, I start to pass some buildings.

The first one is Big Bend's Women's Hockey Association — the brown, boxy arena where every little girl in our village dreams of becoming the next Hayley Wickenheiser. Then there's the Goodwill store and the Salvation Army store — crouched over the sidewalks and facing each other off across the main road like a pair of fat, old sumo wrestlers. Then the infamous Derry's Taxidermy and Cheese Shoppe — during peak season, the massive stuffed moose outside always draws a steady crowd of camera-toting, cheddar-loving cottagers. Even the local villagers can't resist that thing. If you grew up in Big Bend, your parents have a picture stuffed in an album somewhere in their basement of you (with siblings, if you've got 'em) riding Derry's humungous dead moose. Guaranteed.

After a couple more minutes, I arrive at the main strip. But of course, with peak season past, all the businesses along here are dark. After Labour Day, Beachside Books closes at four. Beachy Keen closes at six. Dixie Lee's Ice Cream and Beer Shoppe (yes, we villagers love to use the word "shoppe") closes at nine. Henry's Variety Store shuts down at eleven. The gas station locks up the pumps at midnight. The Spotted Dick (a damp, creaky old British pub) shuts its doors at one. And, yeah, that's pretty much it for our main strip. Told you we're small. But definitely not without charm.

And then I see something up the road that makes my heart skip with hope. I stop in my tracks and stare.

Why didn't I think of it before? Really, it's so obvious. The only place in town where somebody else is guaranteed to be awake like me.

The big, bright orange sign perched on top of our town's shiny new drive-thru burns up the night sky like a flaming piece of cheese (thankfully, with no stuffed dead animals alongside).

McCool Fries.

I aim my sneakers toward it and start jogging.

FOUR

Last April, just before the start of the summer season, our village decided to announce to the world that it was ready to join the big leagues of Canadian tourist destinations. How did it do that, you ask? Elementary, my dear Einstein. By building our very own concrete symbol of modern industry and consumerism, of course.

Yes, I'm talking about a drive-thru snack stand.

And not just a regular old drive-thru: the mayor of Big Bend commissioned a twenty-four-hour drive-thru complete with neon signs, digital menus, and a billboard on Highway 8. Before she died, Aunt Su bet me how long it would take for the drive-thru to go out of business after the tourists and cottagers left for the season. She gave it six months. I gave it four.

Guess no matter what happens now, I win by default.

So here I stand in front of the shiny silver drive-thru speaker, feeling like more of a freak than ever before.

Walking through a drive-thru at the ugliest hour of the night. Why does everything about me have to be so wrong?

I clear my throat and lean close to the microphone. "Um, hello?"

Silence.

I try again, a little louder. "Hello? Anyone there?"

After a couple of seconds, there's a scratchy reply — a voice that sounds like it's crawling out of a yawn.

"Yeah, thanks for choosing McCool Fries. Can I take your order?" Whoever owns the voice sounds surprised and a bit annoyed. Crap, is there a camera on me? Can he see that I don't have a car? My eyes jump around in the darkness, looking for a hidden lens. Yeah, this is probably a serious violation of the drive-thru bylaws. Maybe I should leave.

"Hey, are you going to order something or not?" demands the voice.

My stomach growls painfully as the smell of french fries blows under my nose.

"Um, yeah, okay, I'll have a large fries and a small Coke."

I swear I hear the sound of an exasperated sigh through the static of the speaker.

"That'll be four twenty-five. First window."

Suddenly, I'm regretting this decision. Is this guy going to give me trouble because I woke him up and I don't even have a car? Digging some coins out of my jeans pocket, I walk forward to pay. My palms are sticky with nerves.

The guy slides the window open just over halfway. I can't help myself — I have to stare. He's got the oddest set of features I've ever seen grouped together on one face. His eyes are set widely apart; his nose is long and angular; he's got a birthmark on his cheek, a dimple on his chin, and a top lip that's slightly fuller than the bottom one; and his head is covered with a shaggy mop of brown curls. Strangely enough, the result is a face so good looking that it almost hurts my eyes to look at him. I can hear his music playing softly from behind him — vintage Oasis. He stares at me through narrowed lids. It kind of looks like he's just woken up from a deep sleep and the lights are giving him pain. He must be close to my age, but I don't remember ever seeing him

Deborah Kerbel

in school, which is really bizarre because it's one of those small schools where everybody knows everybody else. His sleepy eyes travel down to my feet and then slowly back up to my face.

"No car?"

I shake my head. *Crap, crap, crap!* Is there enough light for him to see the sudden gush of sweat flooding my upper lip?

"This is a drive-thru, you know?" Is that a smile or a sneer he's trying to hold back?

I shrug, trying my best to look nonchalant (which is French for cool, in case you don't know). "I was out for a walk and I got hungry. Sue me."

"Whatever," he says, reaching out to take my money. I drop the coins into his palm, careful not to touch my slimy, sweaty hands to his smooth, tanned skin. He takes the money and tosses it into the open cash register, like it's garbage he's glad to be rid of. Then he stands up and turns around to get my food. I rise up on my toes to watch him scoop my fries into a bag and pour my caffeine into a cup. The long, toned muscles in his shoulders and back stick out through the thin layer of his cheap polyester uniform. When he turns back to me, my eyes quickly drop to the ground before he can catch me looking.

"Here." It comes out more like a grunt than a word.

Nice. I guess when you look that good, it's easy to get through life without a sparkling personality.

"Thanks." I take a greasy fry from the bag and pop it into my mouth. It's cold and way too heavy on the salt. "Yum," I lie, forcing myself to swallow. "Did you make these?"

"Yeah," he mumbles, reaching out to slide the window closed again with a loud bang. Once I've been nicely shut out, he leans back on his swivel chair, tilts his dimpled chin up to the ceiling, and closes his eyes. I stare at him in complete shock.

Quel rudeness! Sure, the people in our village have their faults, but bad manners isn't one of them. I mean, if you ran a local over with your car, chances are they'd apologize for getting in the way and offer to buy you a cup of tea. Dragging some soda up through the straw, I start to walk across the dark, empty parking lot. My head hangs low as my brain races with questions.

What's that guy's problem? It's like he thinks he's better than me or something! I mean, who exactly does he think he is? Just because you're good looking, doesn't mean you have free licence to be an idiot! Just my luck. The only person awake on this side of the world and he's a total prick.

Now I'm starting to get angry.

Um, have I mentioned yet that I'm prone to great acts of stupidity when I get angry?

Spinning around on my heel, I march back toward the drive-thru, determined to set this guy straight. When I bang on the window, he's so startled he almost falls out of his chair (which gives me more than a small moment of satisfaction).

The window slides open, only a couple of inches this time. The scowl on his face tells me just how pissed he is to have his nap interrupted. "What now?"

Okay, so whatever feeble attempt at customer service he'd been making the first time is officially over and done with.

"I have something to say. Can I come in?" I ask, pointing inside to his crappy little cubicle.

For a second or two, Rude Dude is speechless. And then a streak of anger rolls over his face. It really can't be easy to pull off good-looking and grumpy at the same time, but somehow this guy is able to swing it. If I wasn't so pissed off, I might have been impressed.

"No, you can't come in," he growls, and starts to slam the window again. But I'm faster than he is. I reach out and push my cup of soda onto the track before it can close all the way. The metal frame crushes the cup as it makes contact, splashing the remains of my soda across the counter.

"Look what you did!" he yells, scrambling around for some napkins. But I'm too mad to even think about apologizing.

"You know, just because I don't have a car doesn't give you the right to be so obnoxious," I yell, ignoring the mess of soda pooling in front of me. "Did you know that cars idling at drive-thrus are major contributors to carbon dioxide emissions? Or are you one of those selfish, clued-out idiots who don't give a rat's ass about the environment?"

Yeah, I'm angry now, and the word-vomit is out of my control.

"I mean, you should totally be thanking me for walking through here, you know?" I blabber on. "If anyone should be acting so high and mighty, it should definitely be me. I'm the solution here, not the problem!"

As soon as the words are out of my mouth, I want to stuff them back in.

I'm the solution? Ugh, did I really just say that?

I wait for the inevitable explosion of rudeness. But it doesn't come. For the first time tonight, Rude Dude actually looks awake. And ... is he smiling? *Merde*, does he think that was funny? Or worse, cute? My hands fly up to cover my burning cheeks as I watch him get up from the chair and leave his little room. A second later, a bright red door swings open from the brick building beside me.

"Okay, if you want to talk so badly, come in," he says, motioning me inside with a tilt of his gorgeous head. Yeah, he's definitely smiling. Which just makes him even better looking than before.

Oh man, my pulse is hammering in my ears! Can he hear that?

Sucking in a deep breath, I clutch my bag of icky fries to my chest and walk through the red door. The whole time, the little voice at the back of my brain is screaming out a warning.

Be careful, Lily. What exactly are you getting yourself into?

Which sounds exactly like something my mother would say. Strangely enough, there's a second little voice screaming in my brain too. This one is a bit louder. And it sounds just like Aunt Su.

Yeah, he's hot! You go for it, Lily-girl!

FIVE

Rude Dude leads me into the crappy cubicle, drags out a small stool from under the counter, and motions for me to sit. He leans back in his chair and stretches his long legs out toward me. I can tell right away that the holes in his jeans are the artificial, fancy-designer kind that have been cut and frayed to look cool. My eyes hop around the tiny room as I lower my butt onto the narrow stool. There's a black leather jacket hanging off the back of his chair. The arms of the jacket are so long, the sleeves drag on the dusty floor. In front of the computer monitor, there's a shiny silver iPod hooked up to a small speaker and playing a melancholy British rock tune. Beside it, there's a blank notebook page, a Sharpie pen, and a half-read novel sitting splayed open — in the exact same way Mom always warns me about. *You'll ruin that book's spine, Lily MacArthur.*

I peek at the novel's title. *The Fountainhead* by Ayn Rand. *Why am I not surprised?*

The air in the cubicle feels sticky and damp with cooking oil. And no wonder: the entire far end of the room is taken up with a slick, industrial-sized grill and fryer covered in grease and towering stacks of orange paper containers and bags. The space is so small and cluttered, there's barely room to scratch an itch. I can't imagine spending hours here on my own. Despite all his bad manners, I actually find myself feeling sorry for Rude Dude. Is it actually possible that someone else's nights are worse than mine?

"Okay, you're here," he says, interrupting my thoughts. "So what do you want to talk about so badly?"

Eyebrows arched, he leans forward on the chair to hear my reply. A thin chain dangles out from the V of his uniform shirt collar. There's a solid silver initial ring hanging off the bottom of the chain like a pendant. SB. Somehow, I'm pretty sure those aren't his initials. Just by looking at it, I know the ring is way too small to fit any of his fingers. My mind stretches wide with possibilities. Who does it belong to and why the hell is he wearing it around his neck?

He leans a bit further, and suddenly he's so close I can see the fine, dark hairs of a beard sprouting out through his tanned skin. I take a shaky gulp of air and inhale the smell of toothpaste on his breath.

Cool spearmint — *oh my!*

I'm suddenly hyper-aware of my own breath (did I brush my teeth tonight?) and the little red zit on my chin that I doused with Clearasil just an hour before jumping out my window, and my sticking-out-like-a-chimpanzee ears, and my jagged mess of a haircut from two weeks ago when I tinted it purple and trimmed it in one of those impulsive moments of stupid bravado that inevitably end up in disaster.

And in that instant, every last drop of my earlier courage disappears. The best I can muster up for a reply is a squeaky, teeny-tiny, flower-girl voice.

"Well, I um, kind of said it all out there."

"The emissions thing?"

Nod.

With a bored-sounding sigh, he leans back on his chair again. I have to admit, the little bit of distance is a welcome relief. "Yeah, I heard that too. But that report was actually ripped apart by a later study suggesting that — unless there's a huge lineup of idlers in front of you — parking your car, walking into the restaurant, and then reigniting the engine is probably worse for creating carbon dioxide emissions than driving through. In the future, if you're going to go around spouting science, get it right," he said. "And also, for your information, I bike to work. And everywhere else for that matter. So you can save your whole 'I'm the solution to the problem' bit for someone else."

"Oh." My entire face is burning with a mortified heat. I feel like grabbing one of those paper bags and pulling it down over my head.

"I'm disappointed. For a minute, I thought you actually had something interesting to say. Sure there isn't anything else you wanted to tell me?"

I clear my throat, hoping to scrape the squeak out of my voice. "Well, yeah, you were pretty mean back there. All I was trying to do was order food. Haven't you ever heard that customers are always right?"

"Okay, sorry. You're right."

An awkward silence wraps around the room while Rude Dude scratches his scruffy cheeks and stares at me thoughtfully.

"That all?"

I nod again.

"So if you're done with your little tirade, maybe you could answer a question for me?"

"O-kaaay."

"Tell me what a kid like you is doing up so late at night. It's past four in the morning."

My eyes dive down to the floor as my brain scrambles to come up with something. The truth is too hard to explain and too far out to believe. *I'm a freak who can't sleep and I'll probably be dead in a few days and I don't want to die alone like my Aunt Su so I've been wandering around in the dark looking for company.*

Yeah, sounds pretty lame. And this guy probably wouldn't care anyway. "I ... I just couldn't sleep," I lie. "And it was a nice night, so —"

"So you figured you'd come here and harass the drive-thru attendant?"

My mouth drops open. "I'm harassing *you?*" *Why does it totally feel like it's the other way around?*

The corners of his lips curl down into a frown. "And anyway, aren't you a bit young to be wandering around by yourself in the middle of the night? I mean, don't you have crime rates here? Are small-town people really so ridiculously trusting?"

Man, this guy has some serious charm issues! Suddenly on the defensive, I sit up as tall as I can on that stupid little stool and summon up my most disdainful expression — which isn't as easy as it sounds. Trust me, if you haven't been cursed with shortness, then you have no idea how hard it is to look badass when you're five foot nothing. "I'm almost sixteen, which is plenty old enough to be out at night. And anyway, what about you? Aren't *you* a bit young to be working the graveyard shift in a drive-thru?"

His sleepy, bored voice suddenly turns sharp. "Well, I *am* sixteen. And what I'm doing here is *none of your business.*"

Those last four words come at me like flying circus knives. I have to swallow hard to push down the lump that's rising in my throat. Okay, I can take a hint. Time to change the subject.

"So, is it always this busy around here?"

Shrug.

Unbelievable, now he's pouting like a little kid who got his cookie taken away. I try again. "What do you do in this room all night? Don't you get lonely?"

"I read. And I sleep. At least I try to. Now that the season's over, it's pretty dead. You're my first customer in three days."

"You mean nights."

"Whatever."

I shift my weight on the stool, searching my brain for something interesting to say. Not because I care what he thinks, really. I just don't want to seem like one of those twits from school who gets tongue-tied around good-looking guys.

"So, um, what do your parents say about you working the night shift?"

Ugh, I feel like slapping myself. Just brilliant, twit!

It's obvious my idiocy offends him. His eyes darken at the mention of his parents and his mouth twists into a weird line. "Not much," he snaps, the words landing like a couple of bricks at my feet. And right then and there, I decide it's time to stop asking this guy personal questions. Everything about him is warning me to stop — like he's just slammed the door shut on his personal life.

Cue to exit, Lily!

I rise to my feet, still gripping the bag of uneaten fries. "So, maybe I should just let you go back to your nap?"

"Wait a sec," he says, nodding in the direction of my uneaten food. Dark grease has covered the bottom half of the paper bag, turning the bright orange into a slimy, wet brown. "I just want to say … well, those fries are crap. You don't have to pretend they're any good. I made them about five hours ago." As if to apologize, he takes the bag from my hand and hurls it into the trash can on the other side of the room. He looks at me and shrugs. And in that quick flash of a second, he actually looks kind of guilty. "I shouldn't have sold them to you. I can make you a fresh batch if you want."

What? A fresh batch? Is it possible that just maybe he isn't a total cad? Warmed as I am by the gesture, I have to refuse. "No thanks. I better get going before my mom notices I'm gone and calls the police."

So, just between you and me, that's a lie. Mom would never notice I'm gone because she never wakes up. Neither does Dad, for that matter. My parents are the complete opposite of me (just further proof of my genetic mutation). If they don't get their solid eight hours a night, they get really grumpy and mean. No, Mom isn't going to wake up. But still, I figure it's probably a good idea to end this strange little rendezvous on a high note.

"See you later," I say, pulling open the red door.

"Yeah," Rude Dude replies.

With a wave over my shoulder, I step out into the night. Call me crazy, but it feels like he's actually sorry to see me go.

Maybe that's why I can't resist taking one last peek at him as I walk away from the drive-thru. He's sitting in his chair facing the window and his face is lit up by the neon orange sign shining down from outside. His hands are folded behind his head and he's leaning back with his eyes closed, as if he's already asleep. With his face all calm and peaceful like that, he looks even better than before, and I actually have to stop myself from going back there and knocking on his window again. What is wrong with me? There are plenty of good-looking guys at my school, but I've never gotten so unglued over any of *them* before. What makes this guy so different?

That's when I notice a heavy wristband of silver and gold winking out from beneath his cheap uniform sleeve. *Whoa — nice watch, man!* Even from a distance, I can tell it's expensive. Suddenly, red flags started waving all around my brain. Who exactly is this guy and why is he working the crappiest job known to mankind? iPod, designer jeans, leather jacket, nice watch — he definitely doesn't look like a guy who needs cash this badly. I mean, can you think of a worse job than the graveyard shift at a deserted drive-thru stand in an out-of-the-way village? How does he have such expensive things if he makes minimum wage? Is he some kind of drug dealer? Or maybe the job is a mafia cover. Or maybe he's in the witness protection program and there's a team of highly trained killers on his tail. My imagination swirls with scenarios all the way home as the gravel road Cinammon-Toast-Crunches beneath my shoes.

It isn't until I'm sneaking up the stairs to my bedroom that I realize I didn't even ask his name.

SIX

It wasn't technically what you'd call a daydream. More like a daymare, I guess. I was staring out the kitchen window imagining the details of my upcoming funeral ceremony. Mom and Dad are there, of course, along with my cousin Robert from Rouyn-Noranda, Mr. Duffy, and Ms. Harris, my teacher from last year. That's it. Pretty poor showing, if you ask me. But at least everyone's crying — that's a small consolation. Ms. Harris is particularly sobby. And when she throws herself onto my lowering coffin and wails out a teary apology for the C she gave me in Poetry last year, I can actually feel myself smile through the daymare. Suddenly, Rude Dude walks into the scene and lays a fresh carton of french fries at my grave. He shuffles his feet on the artificial grass and opens his mouth to say something. But I never get the chance to find out what because that's the exact moment when Dad's voice punctures my thoughts.

"Almost forgot — a letter came for you yesterday, Sweetness."

I look up to see him lumbering across the peeling linoleum floor holding the letter and wearing a grin. Quite obviously thrilled to be the bearer of good news. "And it's not a credit card company trying to sell you your first debt-by-plastic. It looks like a real, honest-to-goodness, handwritten letter." My dad is like a giant, overeager puppy sometimes — and most especially on the rare occasions when I come to stay with him. I live with Mom pretty much all the time. I love my dad, but his condo is small and the only bed he has for me is the lumpy pull-out couch in the living room. Not that I really care about comfort, but when you can't sleep, it's nice to have a room of your own to pass the hours. For years, he's been promising to get a bigger place with a proper room for me. But I know that costs a lot of money and my dad's not exactly a billionaire. Even though he works like a dog, when you manage a local non-profit charity there's not much extra room in the paycheque for luxuries like real-estate upgrades. Mom is the money-maker in our family — which is just fine with Dad. Simple things make him happy. I'm pretty sure that if he won the lottery tomorrow, he'd give it all to his charity so he could keep living the way he always has. My dad loves life. Big time. If people were fonts, my dad would be something like **SNAP**. Bold, crisp, and one of a kind.

Dad sinks down into the seat beside me and waves the letter under my nose. The bottle of Tabasco sauce pokes its cap out of his shirt pocket and looks around for something to heat up.

"So, aren't you curious? Who do you think sent it?" He looks so excited about this letter, I almost want to smile. Almost, but not quite enough to actually go through with it. I probably haven't smiled once since Aunt Su died. And I'm definitely not ready to start now.

Pushing away my half-eaten bowl of Shreddies, I stare down at the plain white envelope in his hands. Neat block letters spell out my name and Dad's address in four perfectly straight lines.

Huh. Who on earth would be writing to me?

I take it from him and flip it over, looking for a return address. But the back of the envelope is frustratingly blank. Hopping down from the high kitchen stool, I make for the door.

"Wait, aren't you going to open it?" I hear Dad calling out after me.

"Yeah, once I'm outside."

"Okay, don't be long. Your mom's commanded us to go shopping for school supplies this afternoon. First day's on Monday, remember?"

I can hear the whine around the edges of Dad's voice, but that doesn't stop me for a second. There's no way I'm going to open this letter with an audience. Even though I don't have a clue what's waiting for me inside the envelope, I do know a few key facts.

Fact #1: Everyone under the age of twenty uses email. Stamps and envelopes are so last millennium.

Fact #2: Nobody I know would be sending me a letter. Let's face it, I'm not exactly popular or anything. Aunt Su was my only friend in the world.

Fact #3: Clearly, this letter can't possibly be from her.

I can only conclude that this letter is from some strange old person who isn't my friend. My thoughts flash back to those dusty old ladies from the funeral reception and a shiver centipedes up my spine.

Clutching the envelope, I jog out the front door and down the street as far away as possible from Dad's curious eyes. Once I get to the dog park at the end of the road, I locate the nearest bench and sit down right on the spot next to where the word *bitch* is carved into the fading red-painted wood. My heart is in my throat as I tear open the envelope. Inside are two folded pieces of paper. A white one with the words *to be read first* scrawled on the back in the same neat block letters I'd seen on the envelope. The second piece of paper is leaf-green coloured and sealed closed with a small strip of masking tape. This one also has directions written on the back: *to be read last.*

Quel mystery.

Okay, so I'm not normally much of an order-taker, but in this case I decide to play it safe and go along with the program. Sucking back a long, slow breath of air, I open the white letter and let the words scroll through my brain.

Dearest Lily,

You probably don't know who I am, but I definitely know you. I have, in fact, been hearing all about you since the day you were born. Let me start by saying how sorry I am about your aunt — her death was a devastating loss to anyone lucky enough to know her. I was a great friend of Su's for longer than I can even remember, and the two of us shared many close and personal confidences over the years. This last confidence, however, is by far the most private and meaningful one of all. When Su knew the end was near, she forwarded me the green letter that you are holding in your hands with instructions to mail it directly to your father's address after the funeral. What you're about to read is going to come as a shock, so please be prepared. Before you open it, you must first think of the safest, quietest, most private place you know in the world and then go there. And never forget what a unique and vibrant person your aunt was. And how she loved you more than life itself.

With warm wishes,
Su's friend.

I stare at the letter in my hands for a long time as my mind scrambles to understand. The green letter is from Aunt Su? What exactly did this anonymous friend mean by "when she knew the end was near"? How could she possibly know the end was near?

Her death was a Heath Ledger–style accident. The wrong mixture of prescription meds. Does this idiot not realize that?

I reread the white letter three more times, trying to make sense of what the words mean. What kind of a shock am I in for here? Was Aunt Su secretly married? Or maybe she was an international spy? Or — oh my God — is she still alive and hiding out somewhere completely remote, like a French convent or a cave in the hills of Afghanistan?

All I know for sure is that I have to read Aunt Su's letter if I want to know the truth. The curiosity is scratching my insides raw.

Still clutching both letters, I rise off the bench and start walking away from the dog park. My head is churning with thoughts. The white letter said to go somewhere safe, quiet, and private. Okay, but where? I let my body take over the navigation while my head struggles to prepare itself for what's coming next. To tell you the truth, I don't even know where I'm going or how I'm getting there until I find myself standing in front of Aunt Su's little green lakeside cabin. The clay garden gnome scowls at me from the daisy patch by the front door. I scowl back.

Now, before you go and get the wrong idea, this isn't your regulation cheesy red-capped garden gnome. No, something like that would have been way too generic for my aunt. This garden gnome is bent over with a cigar hanging out of its mouth, pants down around its ankles and mooning everyone who passes with its miniature, hairy gnome butt. It's guaranteed to offend everyone who sees it, which of course was Aunt Su's twisted intention. Mom could never figure out why Aunt Su would want something like that in front of her house. *I ask you, what kind of a person owns a statue like that?* Memories of Mr. Duffy's office flash through my head. *"I do hereby bequeath the entirety of my assets and worldly possessions to my niece, Lily MacArthur."*

Yup, so I guess now the bequeathing little guy belongs to me.

Sidestepping my hairy gnome, I walk around to the back of the cottage. Aunt Su had bought this property decades ago with the money she made from her very first book sale. Back then, it was just a piece of remote, wild land without a house. The way the story goes, she spent that first spring and summer living in a huge tent that she'd pitched by the waterfront, writing furiously on her old manual typewriter. Aunt Su sold her second book by the fall of the same year and had this little cabin built just days before the first snow fell. It was barely four walls and a roof, but she was over the moon to have a place of her own. She didn't even get electricity or running water installed for another ten years. Some people (insert General MacArthur's name here) like to compare it to an overgrown outhouse. But Aunt Su was in heaven here. She loved being alone. Just like me. In all the years she'd lived out here, she hadn't had to deal with any neighbours. There isn't another building around for miles. According to some people (insert Mom's name here, again) it's because nobody wants to look out their windows and see Aunt Su's rambling little "outhouse."

I wind around the rock garden and end up on the back porch. My heart is like an open wound just being here again, but I can't leave. It's the safest, quietest place I know in the world. Reading Aunt Su's letter here feels right.

I sit down on the creaky old glider and run my fingers over the smooth green paper in my lap. What am I about to find inside this letter? What more can Aunt Su possibly have to tell me? My fingers are trembling as I peel back the masking tape and open up the letter. I recognize Aunt Su's handwriting immediately as my eyes land on a little cartoon drawing of an angel diving off the side of a cliff. Aunt Su always drew cartoons in her letters. And there's my own name right underneath, in the exact spot the angel is aiming to fall. Yeah, this is definitely no joke.

Lily-girl,

So here we are, together again for one last chat. Except this time, it'll be a bit one-sided — har-har.

Sorry, stupid joke, right? Guess I'm a bit nervous about all this. I've written a million books, but I've never written my last words before. God, this is harder than I thought. Okay, I think the first thing I want to say is how badly I feel to have left you high and dry like this. I never planned to die on you this soon, but sometimes life messes up our plans, you know? Something I never told you is that I've been sick for a long time. Years, actually. Only a couple of people knew this, but I'm not about to apologize for keeping that secret. If there's one thing I just can't stand, it's pity. And so, when I found out last month that my cancer was back stronger than ever (stage four terminal, they call it), I made a harsh decision. Lily, you know I'm the kind of gal who's always known exactly how she wanted to live her life. And once I knew it was all about to come to a really ugly end, I decided to rewrite that manuscript to one that suited me better. I just hope one day you'll come to understand why I made the choice I did.

These words are like a kick in the face. I want desperately to close my eyes and stop reading. But I can't. I just have to know the rest. Taking a deep breath, I force my eyes down the rest of the page.

I know you're going to be sad about losing me, but I want you to pull yourself together and get over it. You're too young to waste your time crying over a crazy old bat like me. Yes, the nights are going to be hard, but trust me, all those extra hours of life are a gift. And now that I'm gone maybe you'll finally get around to using it. You're destined for amazing things — I've known it since the day you were born. You're going to make a big difference in someone's life. This is something I know for sure.

Oh God, how I'm going to miss you, my Lily-girl! You were, without doubt, the brightest and shiniest part of this long and colourful life.

Su

P.S. I know your mother is keeping you away from my place. Even in death, she probably thinks I'm a terrible influence. There's an extra key to my cottage inside the garden gnome. Go whenever you need a place to be alone or think of me. And help yourself to any of my books. Remember, every writer is a reader first.

P.P.S. Have you figured out what to do with my ashes yet? No? Don't worry, I know you'll come up with the perfect place.

By the time I get to the end of the page, I feel like someone has just drilled a bloody, gaping hole through my chest. As I struggle to suck air into my lungs, my brain tries to make sense of Aunt Su's letter.

Why I made the choice I did ... rewrite the manuscript to one that suited me better ...

Merde! Does this mean what I think it means? I read it again and again, each time searching for a different truth. But the sick reality of what she did is unmistakeable. My tears splash down onto the green paper, blurring Aunt Su's suicide note into a soggy, illegible mess. It doesn't really matter if I can't read it anymore — her words are permanently tattooed onto my brain. With a scream so screeching loud that the force of it burns up my throat, I crumple the letter into an angry ball and hurl it to the porch floor. I bury my teary face in my hands and sob like a person who's lost everything in the world. 'Cause I have.

How could you do this to me, Aunt Su? HOW COULD YOU DO THIS TO ME?

Time must still be passing, but I really have no idea how long I sit there on that glider, crying myself into a wet, snotty mess. Thank God there are no neighbours near enough to hear me, because the last thing I want is for someone to come and see me or, even worse, try to comfort me.

When there are no tears left, I sit up and stare at the crumpled letter at my feet. I suddenly feel so worn out and tired, I can almost imagine sleeping. But mostly I feel empty, like my insides have been scooped out of my body and tossed into the lake.

A slimy, gutted fish.

Sweeping the balled-up letter off the floor, I stand up and walk down to the edge of the lake. I march out to the end of Aunt Su's funny circular dock, open up the crumpled letter, and shred it into pieces. And then when the pieces are too small to tear anymore, I hurl them into the water. They're really too tiny to fly very far. A few little green bits float down to my feet while the rest land in the shallow water right in front of the dock, floating on the surface like mini fallen leaves.

You are destined for amazing things. What the hell does that mean? Despite my anger, I almost want to laugh. Please! Reading too many fortune cookies lately? I mean, what am I supposed to do with that? And how exactly am I going to make a difference in somebody's life? Change the world? End poverty? Stop wars? It's quite possibly the dumbest thing I've ever heard! I can't believe I looked up to this woman for so many years! How dare she decide to go and kill herself and leave me with the weight of the stupid world on my shoulders? I'm not destined for amazing things! I can't even sleep!

I stare out across the water. The touristy motorboats and wave riders have all vanished for the year and the surface is smoother today than I've ever seen it, like a hundred acres of soft, grey velvet. I feel the sudden urge to lie down in it, close my eyes, and let it cover me up like a blanket. If I did that, sleep certainly would follow.

Forever sleep.

Without a second's hesitation, I throw myself into the lake and start splashing away from the dock. The water's shallow at first, but the bottom begins to fall away after a couple of minutes. Soon enough, it's up to my chin, and then covering my eyes, and then over my head. But I keep moving forward. I open my eyes under water; the grey velvet blinds me. I open my mouth and let out a wet scream that steals every last molecule of air from my lungs. I hold myself down, fighting the instinct to rise up and breathe. I want to smother this giant feeling of anger. I want to feel like myself again. I want to numb this pain. I want to go to sleep. Right here, right now, in Aunt Su's lake.

My lungs begin to burn and the muscles in my limbs spark and tingle. I fight to keep my body from floating to the surface. The numbness begins to take over my brain. It feels lovely, like a long-lost friend. An image of Aunt Su and her beautiful, crinkly face passes in front of my open eyes. I can almost hear her voice again, moving in my ears somewhere beyond the swish of the water. Her voice, calling my name through the pulse of the waves. I miss her so badly, I want to die. I want to drown myself in this lake and never feel a moment of pain again. But then I think of the choice Aunt Su made and the anger begins to grow inside my stomach again. How *dare* she send herself off to sleep forever and leave me terminally awake? How could she be so selfish?

Suddenly re-energized by anger, I don't want to die anymore. Instead, I push my feet against the soft bottom of the lake and rise up for air. The first breath is like a knife pushing down my throat. I take another. And then another. The sweet numbness retreats from my brain. All that's left is the anger.

With tears blurring my eyes, I drag myself out of the lake and run back to the road. My wet shoes squish and croak like swamp frogs with each step. When I pass the mooning garden gnome on my way off the property, I slow my steps down just long enough to give it a good, hard kick in the ass.

SEVEN

September 9th

Grade ten is just millimoments away from starting.

Merde sandwich!

The first day back at school always blows big time. But for some reason, adults always expect us to be excited at the idea of getting back to school. When in fact the reality is, unless you're a cheerleader, a browner, or a clueless, drugged-out motorhead, it's the worst day of the year. And for me, this year is shaping up to be worse than any other. Facing high school with no friends is one thing. But doing it on zero sleep, under the umbrella of certain death, just two weeks after the most important person in your life secretly offed herself is indescribably heinous.

I take the long way to school, delaying the inevitable as long as possible. Today I'm feeling more like a ghost than a girl. My feet make their way down the sidewalks and across the streets like they're on autopilot, but the entire time my head is completely lost in my thoughts. For two days and two nights now, I haven't been able to get Aunt Su's letter out of my head. Not even for a second.

You are going to make a big difference in someone's life.

What does that mean? Really. I'm just a sleepless kid from a village that dreams of being a town. How is someone like me going to make a difference? I mean, does she think I'm going to use these long night hours to change the world or something?

Outside the school, kids are hanging together in small, mostly blond groups. All the exact same cliquey formations from last year — as if the past three months haven't even happened. Avoiding eye contact with all of them, I duck around the corner from the chattering crowd and squat down on the pavement, waiting for the first bell to ring.

So in case you haven't realized it yet, I'm kind of what you'd call *the odd girl out*. And not just at school. I'm the odd girl out pretty much everywhere I go. Never been part of any group and never really wanted to be. My mom likes to tell people I'm shy. She thinks it makes me sound halfway normal. I hate it when she does that. "Shy" is a lame way to try to make me sound like a person who's afraid of other people. I'm not afraid of other people. I just prefer my own company. "Introvert" is a much better word for someone like me. Aunt Su always used to warn me that the world will interpret introversion as snobbery, so I'd better get used to a snooty reputation. She knew that from first-hand experience.

Lucky for me, I usually don't care what other people think.

"Hey, Lily."

See? I'm so used to being left alone that, for a second, I don't even realize someone is talking to me.

"Lily?" the voice tries again, a little louder this time.

I look up, shielding my eyes from the bright morning sun. Emma Swartz is standing in front of me, hands awkwardly gripping the straps of her backpack. Her red hair bounces over her freckled shoulders in a series in perfect spirals.

"Hey," I say. It sounds more like a question than a reply. Except for that one time at Aunt Su's cabin, Emma and I haven't spoken two words to each other since I snuck away from her birthday party and pulled the arms off her Barbie doll collection in senior kindergarten. *Why is she talking to me now?*

She shuffles her flip-flopped feet against the cement. Her toenails are painted almost the exact same shade as her hair. Just a couple of gradients on the colour wheel away from Beet It.

"I just wanted to say ... you know ... sorry about your aunt dying. That really sucks. She seemed really nice ...you know ... I used to see her in my dad's store sometimes."

Emma's father owns our village's only bookstore, Beachside Books. He used to invite Aunt Su in for author visits every once in a while. Remembering this now, my defences lower slightly.

"Thanks," I mumble, blinking hard to kill the stinging in my eyes. *Okay, you've said sorry. You can leave now.*

But, apparently, Emma has more she needs to get off her chest.

"Yeah, every time she came to the store, she used to draw crazy cartoons of herself inside her novels. Always a different one in each book."

She smiles as she speaks about Aunt Su, making her braces glitter in the sunlight. Against all my better judgement, I feel myself softening a bit.

"Yeah, she liked doing stuff like that," I say, thinking about the funny little sketches she'd drawn inside my birthday cards every year. The one from my last birthday is the best — it's a picture of me and Aunt Su lying awake under a field of purple and green stars, making faces at the man on the moon. Since the day she died I've been passing the nights with it right next to my bed, hoping it'll somehow help me get to sleep. And then I think about the angel drawing from her suicide note and my insides turn back to cement.

"So anyways," Emma continues, "I just wanted to tell you that ... well, I always thought your aunt was pretty cool."

Yeah, I thought so too, until she killed herself and abandoned me. I can feel an angry scream start to rise in my throat, but I push it back down. Don't need to expose my freak around this school any more than I already have.

"Thanks," I say instead.

"By the way, I like the purple."

"Huh?"

Emma lets out a funny, snorty kind of laugh. It sounds so much like a backward sneeze that I almost say *gesundheit.* "You know, in your hair? It's awesome."

My hands fly up to my jaggedy head. I almost forgot about the colour treatment I put in.

"Thanks. I did it myself."

"Really?" She sounds genuinely impressed. "Maybe you'll show me how sometime?"

I don't know what to say to that. Next thing, she'll be inviting me over to do our nails and watch *High School Musical.* I can feel my defences creeping back up again. That's when the first bell rings, mercifully saving me from any more attempts at small talk.

"See ya 'round," I say, happy to pull myself up off the pavement and make my escape into the school. Pushing my way through the crowd, I head straight to class so I can snag one of the choice seats in the back of the room. The seat you get on the first day is almost always the one you end up with for the rest of the semester, so it's vital to choose wisely. But when I walk through the door of my homeroom, my heart sinks to the floor. I'm too late — the entire back three rows are already claimed. Half blind with irritation, I slump into an empty third-row seat, silently cursing myself for getting caught up with chit-chatty Emma and not getting here on time.

The second bell rings out, cutting through the buzz of excited voices and warning us to shut our traps. Our homeroom teacher rises to his feet, holding a crumpled piece of paper in his left hand. Mr. Becker. All the kids call him Pecker behind his back. He's our pervy phys. ed. instructor from last year who used to leer at all the pretty girls in their skimpy school-issued gym shorty-shorts. Even though it went against the official dress code, I always wore black leotards under my pair. As a result, after a full ten months of daily dodge ball and badminton sessions, I don't think he even knows my name. Not that he'd leer at me anyway. I don't think I'm the kind of girl pervy gym teachers look at that way.

As soon as the anthem is over, Pecker ambles to the front of the room, a painful smile glued to his face. He's one of those old men who always look like they're holding back a fart. You know the type.

"Welcome back to the start of another year. For those of you who don't know me, my name is Mr. Becker." I groan inwardly. *For those of you who don't know me?* What is he talking about? The exact same group of kids has been going to this school since junior kindergarten. Who doesn't know Pecker?

"We'll start with attendance, and then I'll pass around the seating plan, locker assignments, and class schedules," he continues. "But before we begin, I'd like to introduce a brand new student." He pauses here, as if to let the effect of this announcement sink in.

"That's right, a new student. Mr. Benjamin Matthews will be joining us this year, all the way from Upper Canada College in Toronto."

The classroom chatter drops a little in volume while everyone looks around to locate the private school newbie. Everyone except me, that is. New kids in our midst are a rare occurrence. But inevitably they turn out to be as dull as the rest of the nitwits around this place.

"Says here that last year, Benjamin was ... let's see ..." Pecker pauses for a second to consult the crumpled mess in his hand.

"... the editor of his high school's newspaper, the treasurer of his student council, and the vice-president of his Junior Achievement executive team. I'm hoping that means we can expect great things from him at Big Bend High. Benjamin, would you stand up so we can all see who you are? People, please help me welcome him to our school."

My ears twitch with intrigue at the word *editor*. Is this new kid a writer like me? It's almost enough to get me excited. I've never met anyone else my age who wanted to be a writer. But when a familiar voice speaks from behind me, rising just slightly above the drone of conversation, the hairs on the back of my neck stand up on end. It's a voice so bored, I know right away it can only belong to one person.

"It's Ben. Just Ben," the voice says.

An invasion of shivers lands on my skin. I think I actually stop breathing.

So.

Rude Dude has a name.

I blink slowly and whisper the name so quietly, it sounds like a breath.

Ben.

Only three letters, but it explodes in my mouth like a handful of Pop Rocks chased with cola.

EIGHT

I catch up to him on the way out of homeroom. His legs are so long, I have to jog to match his pace. "Hey!" I say, reaching out to poke him in the arm. "Remember me?"

He glances at me for a nanosecond and keeps walking.

"Yeah, I remember."

"I didn't know you were going to this school, Ben," I try again. I know it's dumb, but I'm excited for the chance to say his name out loud.

The Pop Rocks don't disappoint.

Unlike his reply.

"Yeah, well now you do," he says, his voice just as bored as ever.

"Looks like we're in the same homeroom," I blab on, starting to pant from the exertion of running, "so I don't mind showing you around if you want."

I trot after him, waiting for his answer. For the life of me, I can't remember a time I've ever actually initiated a conversation in this school, let alone ran after one. What's my problem? Why am I trying so hard with this guy? Was it the "editor" thing? Or because he seems different from the others around here? Or is it just because he's good looking? What kind of shallow *salope* am I turning into?

As it turns out, it doesn't really matter what variety of shallow *salope* I am, because instead of replying, Ben just ignores me and keeps walking, hands stuffed deep into his pockets like he's digging for gold. He doesn't even look at me once. As soon as I begin to decelerate from a jog to a walk, he speeds ahead down the hall until he's lost in the crowd.

I slow to a full stop and watch him disappear.

Quel snob!

"Hey, do you know that guy?" asks a voice beside me. I turn around to see Emma Swartz staring at me, an expression of wide-eyed shock slashed across her freckled face.

Her again? What's going on with me? First day back at school and already I've smashed my yearly conversation record by a kilometre.

"Not really. I've just seen him working at the drive-thru."

"McCool Fries?" her brown eyes light up at the mention of greasy fast food. "You work there?"

I shake my head. "Not me, him." I can't quite bring myself to say his name in front of her. Just in case she notices the Pop Rocks go off. "He works the night shift."

"Wait a minute: Ben Matthews works at the drive-thru?" Her eyes are bugging out of her head, like it's the most far-fetched concept she's ever heard. "That's a joke, right?"

"No. Why? What's so funny about it?"

She shrugs. "Nothing, I guess. I just never got the impression that a guy like him needed the money."

Now it's my turn to look shocked. "What does that mean? Do you *know* him?"

"Well, not really. His family has a summer cottage here and I've just seen him a few times down at the Docks with all his fancy city friends. He's the kind of guy a girl notices, right?" She raises her eyebrows suggestively.

My face burns at this.

So. Completely. Mortifying.

Anxious for an escape, I pick up my feet and start walking to my next class. Emma follows along behind me. Man, why is she suddenly so interested in talking to me? My introverted self is beginning to freak out more than just a little.

As it turns out, Emma follows me all the way to the door of my first class — advanced trig with Ms. Pinski. Okay, I admit I'm a bit of a browner myself when it comes to numbers. Math and science have always come pretty easily for me. And I'm a natural at trigonometry — a subject most kids in my grade find next to impossible. Maybe I'm so good at it because ... well, because I'm all about angles myself. Seriously, to look at me, you'd see a square face sitting on top of a rectangular body. Even my hair falls in perfect straight lines, like each strand has been carefully drawn by a ruler. If people were fonts, I would be Arial. Scratch that: I would be Arial Narrow. Guess you could say I'm the opposite of curve.

Which, as you probably know, isn't exactly a great look for high school.

"Whoa, killer math, dude," Emma groans, veering away from me. "I'm heading over to French."

"Good. Say hi to that *connard* Monsieur Zeitoune for me."

You've probably noticed by now that I love swearing in French. A few years ago, my second cousin from Rouyn-Noranda came to stay with Aunt Su for a summer. Robert taught me all the really choice French curses, which turned out to be really useful. If you know someone who speaks French, I highly recommend it. Learning those words was the only nice thing about having to share Aunt Su's company with Robert for an entire six weeks. French curses give such a satisfying air of mystery to the simplest and dirtiest of English words ... kind of like turning puke into pearls. *N'est-ce pas?*

For some reason, though, Emma doesn't look too impressed with my linguistic prowess. "Okay. Later."

Her round derriere swings from side to side as she sashays off down the hall. Apparently angles and ratios are not for Emma. If people were fonts, she would be Curlz. Without a doubt. Maybe it's rude, but I can't help letting out a loud sigh of relief as I watch her go. So far, this morning has been *way* too social for comfort. Can't say I'm sorry to see it end.

Hitching my backpack up on my shoulders, I open the door to my trig class and scan the room for a good seat. That's when, for the second time in one morning, my heart does a kamikaze into my stomach.

Not again!

Only three spots left open: two smack dab in the front row and one in the dead centre of the room ... right behind *Ben Matthews*. Darn that Emma! Somehow she's managed to mess up my back-row plans twice in under an hour! Since I'm not about to get stuck in front-row hell, I opt for the lesser of two evils and slide into the chair behind His Grumpiness. If Ms. Pinski is as anal about seating plans as the rest of the teachers in this school, I'll be staring at the back of his swelled head every day for the rest of the semester.

Completely made of suck!

Still angry, I slink down low in my seat, crushing my lips together to keep them from spouting out any more embarrassments. If Ben notices me sitting behind him, he doesn't let on. As soon as the bell rings, Ms. Pinski closes the door and passes around a class seating plan for us to fill out. I cringe as I add my name to the empty box underneath Ben's. How can someone who looks so nice on the outside be so ugly on the inside? Because as much as it pains me to admit it, he *does* look nice.

I sigh softly, breathing in the fresh smell of Ben's shampoo.

Watermelon. Yum. While Ms. Pinski drones on about functions and ratios, I notice how his shoulders rise up with each of his breaths. How the bottom of his hair curls every so slightly around the collar of his T-shirt. How his head is tilted ever so slightly to the left. And how every few seconds it tilts a little bit further and further ...

Suddenly, a soft rumbling sound fills my ears and a little light switch flips on inside my head. Oh my God, Ben's taking a nap! Just like that night at the drive-thru! I'm about to kick his chair and wake him up, when the sound of Ms. Pinski's voice rings out over our heads. And it definitely doesn't sound amused.

"Benjamin Matthews?"

His neck snaps straight up like a rubber band.

"Yeah, uh, here."

A chorus of snickers bounces around the room. Ms. Pinski smirks in a self-satisfied "spider about to catch the fly" kind of way.

"Are you *really*, Mr. Matthews? I'm not so sure about that. Maybe you could prove it by repeating my last question for the rest of the class?"

"Yeah, I ... uh ..."

There's only the slightest hint of boredom left in his voice as he scrambles for the answer. Maybe it's because he looks just as tired as *I* should look. Or maybe it's because I know how crappy it is to have to stay up all night. I really don't know why, but part of me suddenly feels sorry for him. Even if he is a rude, arrogant son of a Mafioso drug dealer. I guess I take after Dad — both of us are suckers for people in need of help.

So, against all my better judgment, I find myself leaning forward and whispering the answer in his ear.

"She's looking for the mathematical definitions of sine and cosine."

I can see Ben's shoulders bristle at the sound of my voice. And then he gives his head a vigorous little shake, almost like he's trying to evict me from his thoughts. His chair scrapes back with a screech as he rises to his feet.

"I'm sorry, I didn't hear your question, Ms. Pinski. I must have fallen asleep. It won't happen again."

I feel like I've just been slapped across the face. Why didn't he take the answer I gave him? Does he think he's too good to accept help from someone like me? My cheeks flash with shame as the rest of the class erupts into nervous giggles around me.

"Sleeping in my class? Not the best way to make a first impression, Mr. Matthews. Take your seat and let's continue. Because it's the first day, I'll let it slide. Just don't let me catch you doing it again!"

Well, I'm not planning on being quite so forgiving. I spend the rest of the hour cursing Ben Matthews in my head and plunging imaginary arrows into his back. What an ungrateful, pigheaded snob! Who does he think he is?

I work myself up into such a tizzy over the whole thing that I can't even concentrate on the rest of the math lesson. By the time the bell rings, my heart is fluttering like a leaf in a windstorm. And when I stand up, my knees wobble and a cluster of stars explodes in front of my eyes. I clutch the back of my chair for support and take a couple of slow, deep breaths. But it doesn't help. My heart still feels like it's trying to fly out of my chest. I've never let myself get so upset over a guy before. What's going on?

That's when it hits me.

It's been fourteen days (nights) since I've had any sleep.

This is it.

My heart is giving out.

Je suis fini.

And without even making it into the Guinness book.

Merde.

I have to get help.

Now.

Muscling past the crowd of kids, I rush down the hall to the nurse's office.

"Call an ambulance, Ms. Green!" I gasp, staggering through the door. "I need help!"

The nurse glances up from her book and eyes me suspiciously.

"Lily MacArthur! What are you up to?"

"Please," I cry, my voice rising in panic. "I'm pretty sure it's cardiac arrest."

With a sharp cluck of her tongue, she points me to a creaky little cot and reaches for her stethoscope. I collapse into a quivering ball of Jell-o while she takes my pulse and feels my glands. After a minute, she pops the stethoscope tips into her ears. I squeeze my eyes shut and prepare for the worst. At this point, I'm so far gone I can't even feel the fluttering anymore. Instead, a tight, burning pain has taken its place and is rapidly spreading down my arms and up into my throat.

"And what did you have for breakfast this morning?" she asks, dragging the chilly metal disk over my chest.

My eyes fly open. "Excuse me?"

"Did you have any coffee? Or some kind of energy drink?"

I stare at her in surprise. "No! What's that supposed to —"

She holds up a finger to her lips, indicating for me to be quiet. Seconds tick by while I consider telling her about my missing sleep. I wonder if that's the kind of vital information she should know about just in case I fall unconscious before the paramedics arrive. But before I can say anything else, she pulls the stethoscope tips out of her ears and sighs.

"I don't hear anything wrong with your heart, Lily. I think you just experienced a palpitation."

I prop myself up on an elbow. "A what?"

"Palpitation. They're quite common and completely harmless. Probably due to a bad case of first-day jitters."

On the tail of these words, the tight, burning pain in my upper body dissolves away to numbness. All that's left is the awkward heat in my cheeks as Ms. Green reaches into the pocket of her white lab coat and pulls out a pink lollipop.

"Here you go."

"Are you serious? That's it?"

"I suppose if it happens again, you might want to mention it to you family doctor. But really, I wouldn't worry." She stands up, opens the door, and waves me out of the room. "Off you go. Back to class."

Nice. I'm dying and nobody gives a toss. Now I'm really glad I didn't tell her about my sleep crisis. She probably wouldn't have believed that either. Ignoring her stupid lollipop, I scuttle out of the room and down the hall.

Man, didn't I tell you the first day back at school always blows?

NINE

September 12th

The absolute bottomless black hole of the night is back again. But tonight, I'm not planning on waiting around for it to suck me into its evil vortex.

I swing my legs around the open window sill and let my feet hover for a moment above the landing pad of soft grass below. It's now been seventeen days since I've slept. Well, seventeen nights actually. Just two days (nights) away from breaking the world record. Somebody get the Guinness people on the phone! Wonder what kind of proof they're going to need to make it official? Would an autopsy report of my exhausted brain cells do? I close my eyes and choke back an angry sob.

Lately, I feel like a death row prisoner waiting for the electric chair to juice up. My eyes sweep over my room and land on Aunt Su's pomegranate jar-of-death. I still haven't figured out what to do with it yet. And unless I catch some serious zees soon, I'm going to run out of time. The General keeps harping on me, talking about how unsanitary it is to keep human remains in my room and how she doesn't want ashes hanging around her house much longer. Between you and me, I think she'd be happy if I just flushed them down the toilet along with my morning dump. That way, she could finally be rid of her eccentric half-sister forever. I lean over as a wave of cramps pass through my stomach — I swear, that thought just made my insides turn to goulash.

Once the nausea's passed, I run back into the room and pull the jar off the desk. *You're coming with me tonight, Aunt Su.* Cradling the pomegranate in my arms, I hop back onto the window ledge, push off from the sill, sail through the air, and land with a rolling thud on the long grass below. As soon as I catch my breath, I look up to locate the moon. It's resting on the treetops, a pale half-circle hanging in the sky. Like an empty cereal bowl waiting to be filled with Frosted Flakes and milk.

My stomach gurgles at the thought, but I ignore it and take off down the road with Aunt Su tucked under my arm like a football. This time, I know exactly where I'm headed. And it isn't McCool Fries. Believe you me. Where am I going? I'll give you a clue: I'm heading to the one place in the world where I'm positive my sleep is hiding out. Yup, I'm happy to report that my exhausted brain cells have finally solved the answer to that mystery.

Want another clue? Okay, fine, last one: if General MacArthur catches wind of this little field trip of mine, she'll have a big, horny cow. That's right, my sleep has been kidnapped by an evil zombie dude and is currently bound, gagged, and tied to a chair in a dark corner of Aunt Su's cabin.

Okay … not really. So I know my sleep isn't actually being held hostage at Aunt Su's place. But being around her stuff *has* to help me find it again, dontcha think?

Worth a shot, at least. At this point, I'm seriously running out of options.

So there I am, walking down the dark road and scanning through the beam of my flashlight for something amazing to do. But all I can see are some random piles of trash lying by the grassy curb. A few soda cans, a cigarette pack, and a ripped plastic bag. I pick them up and carry them with me until I pass a garbage can. I guess cleaning up the streets is a start, but not a very good one. Definitely not amazing. Village custodial maintenance can't possibly be what Aunt Su means for me to be doing, can it? If I really want to make a difference, maybe I should be looking for a solution to world hunger. I mean, if I can get General MacArthur going off on one of her stress kicks, she could probably force-feed the world.

Le sigh.

I feel like my life is a giant jigsaw puzzle and I'm missing the most important piece. And, don't ask me to explain why, but I have the strongest feeling the missing piece is back at Aunt Su's cabin. Like maybe if I do something amazing, I get to stay alive? My flashlight wavers as I crest the last gravelly hill leading to the cabin. As you've probably guessed, my anger has mellowed a bit since my last visit there. Let's face it — there's really not much use being furious with a dead person. At this point, almost all that rage has settled into an overdose of sadness — a thousand dripping tears slowly eroding away at my guts like some pathetic form of Chinese water torture.

Next thing I know, I'm standing in the driveway staring at Aunt Su's little wooden shack. It looks smaller and thinner than ever before. And it's leaning a few degrees to the left, like it's tired and needs to lie down.

A sandstorm of nerves whips through my guts. This is going to be my first time inside Aunt Su's cabin since she died. It's going to hurt bad. I can feel my muscles start to tighten with anticipation. Before going in, I decide to head down to the little herb garden on the south wall to gather up some mint leaves. A cup of Moroccan Nana tea should help loosen my muscles and calm my nerves. It always does. Aunt Su used to make it for me whenever I got upset.

Oh God! *Aunt Su.*

I put the pomegranate down beside a swaying marijuana plant. The tears start forming even before I pick the first sprig of mint. The fresh, sweet smell is so powerful it manages to bring my dead aunt rushing back to me in a flood of memories. On the weekends when Mom let me stay over here at the cabin, Aunt Su would stay up most of the night with me. Sometimes, we'd just skip sleep entirely and talk until the sun came up. We'd sip on steaming cups of tea, curl up on the couch, and talk about everything you can imagine. She'd tell me about all the cities she'd visited in her life. She'd tell me about every person who'd ever betrayed her, every time she'd ever been in love, and every big adventure she'd woken up to find herself stuck in the middle of. And we'd talk about me. Aunt Su would always tell me how lucky I was — how I was getting to live a longer life than most people since I didn't need to sleep as much of it away. We'd talk a lot about writing. She'd look through my scribbling stories and let me tap away on her laptop (yes, she'd finally upgraded her old manual typewriter to a MacBook) and listen to my dreams of growing into a writer just like her one day. She'd tell me the names of all her favourite authors and read excerpts from some of her favourite books and poems. *Every writer is a reader first, Lily-girl. Keep reading, and one day I'll be putting your books up on those shelves.*

I drop to my knees in the dirt and let my tears pour out. I cry for the horrible image of Aunt Su ending her life all alone in her bed. And how I didn't get the chance to be there to hold her hand when she slipped away forever. I cry at the awfulness of never getting to say goodbye. I cry for the fact that I'll never hear her voice again. I cry for the picture of her face in my head that's getting blurrier with every day. I cry for the canyon of emptiness inside me that's never going to be filled. I cry for my missing sleep. And the death sentence that's hanging over my head.

Once the herb garden has been watered thoroughly with tears, I wipe my face with the sleeve of my hoodie, pull myself back up to my feet, pick up the pomegranate jar, and go get the key. The obscene little gnome is waiting for me in his usual spot. I grab him and flip him upside down. There's a teeny round hole carved out at the bottom of his pointy gnome shoes. With one big shake, the cabin key clatters loose and lands at my feet. I pick it up and open the door quickly, before I can change my mind. Stepping inside, I flip on the ceramic elephant lamp Aunt Su had brought back from her last trip to Thailand and peer around the main room. Everything looks exactly the same as it always did. Truly. For a split second, I half expect Aunt Su to walk out of her bedroom wearing her favourite purple kimono. Comfy clothes, she always called the drawer full of nightshirts and bathrobes she liked to wear when she was writing.

"You got to be comfortable so the words can flow smoothly from your head to your fingertips," she'd say. "Ideally, every writer would work naked. Think of all the incredible ideas that would help to release into the world. You know I'd go commando all day long if I didn't catch a chill so easily."

And I knew she would, too. She was just that wingding-ish.

Suddenly, out of the shadows I hear a rustling noise coming from the direction of Aunt Su's bedroom. My heart freezes. *Oh my God! What's that?* And then the craziest thought skips through my head.

Maybe they're wrong. Maybe she's not dead. Maybe they cremated an empty casket and Aunt Su has been hiding out in her cabin this whole time, laughing hysterically about the big joke she's played on the world. *Har-har. Gotcha good, Lily-girl!*

I wouldn't put it past her. Nervously, I lift the lid of the pome-granate jar and peer inside. But it's too dark to tell if there are actually ashes in there or not.

"Um, hello?" I whisper, replacing the lid and taking a baby step forward. "Is somebody here?"

One more small step and I'm inching open the bedroom door. The hinges reply with a long wavering creak. Another rustle and then a trio of teeny brown mice run scurrying away from the light. My heart slowly goes back to normal speed. *Just a few rodents. Relax!*

I sweep my eyes over the snarl of stuff in Aunt Su's room. The collection of Inuit soapstone statues collecting dust on top of her mahogany dresser, the teetering wall-to-wall shelves of paperback romance novels, the futon with its leaf-coloured sheets, all crumpled up in the middle of the mattress like a giant discarded green tissue. I reach out to straighten them but stop. Aunt Su never made her bed once in the fifteen and a half years I knew her. Seems only right to leave it be.

Pulling the mint leaves out of my hoodie pouch, I head over to the kitchen to make myself a cup of Nana tea. On the way, I sidestep the obstacle course of scattered stuff that makes up Aunt Su's decor. The wooden black rhino carving she liked to use as a footstool, her pile of stuffed frogs (not the fuzzy kind — these frogs were of the Derry's Taxidermy and Cheese Shoppe persuasion), the tangled garden of overgrown indoor plants (which were now completely keeled over with thirst), the eclectic mishmash of furniture collected from garage sales and antique markets, and, of course, more teetering bookshelves reaching up to nudge the ceiling. To call this place cluttered would be an understatement. Funny, the clutter was never so obvious to me as it is now. Guess I never paid too much attention to all the crazy stuff before; it was just part of the eccentric background that was Aunt Su's home. But tonight every single piece of it seems to have fallen out of context. Without Aunt Su here, none of this stuff makes any kind of sense anymore. Like the whole collection has lost the one thing that used to tie it together.

All this eccentric bequeathing stuff.

All of it mine now.

The kitchen is at the back of the cabin, adjacent to the wall of windows that looks out onto the lake. All of the windows in Aunt Su's cabin are bare. When she had this place built, her one request was lots of big, naked windows. "Artists need light. And lots of it," she used to say. "Curtains are a waste of money when you've got a view like this." I remember once asking if the lack of privacy ever bothered her. "There's no one around for miles. What do I need privacy for? So nobody sees me writing my next book? Or dancing around in my birthday suit?"

"What about the weed? Aren't you worried about someone seeing that? It's illegal, you know."

"Not when you have a prescription," she said, turning her face away from the light.

At the time I didn't understand what that meant, and she didn't offer to explain.

Think I just figured it out. It's legal for cancer patients.

Behind me, I can hear the kettle rushing and racing into a high-pitched whistle, like an oncoming train. I make the tea, drop in some mint leaves, and bring the steaming cup to my mouth. My eyes sting from the burn of the steam, but it feels good. In a weird way, it helps to take my mind off the pain coming at me from inside.

One burning sip.

Another.

Better.

Cradling the cup in my hands, I let my eyes creep over the room again. God, what am I going to do with all this stuff? There's a fine layer of dust covering the furniture and nests of cobwebs draping the upper corners of the room. Aunt Su was never much of a housekeeper. If she wasn't writing or riding her moped, she was spending time with me. Cleaning was never very high on her priority list. I don't even think she owned a broom, unless it was to chase away the mice. I could probably empty the pomegranate out right here in this room and nobody would even notice the difference. Yeah, those ashes would blend in perfectly with all the dust. But that doesn't seem right. No, there's got to be a better spot for them.

Eventually, my eyes come to a stop on the bookshelf nearest to me. Putting down the tea, I wander over and find the shelf with Aunt Su's books. Shoshanah M. Chase. That was her pen name. I slide my fingers along the row of titles.

Thump, thump, thump over the long line of spines. There are dozens of them. Had I ever paid attention to how many books she'd written? There's a virtual library of Aunt Su's words here. I'm suddenly overwhelmed with the urge to read one. Maybe just hearing her words in my head will bring back my sleep.

My fingers pause on a spine that's sticking out slightly from the otherwise neat row. The title swirls with green and purple letters. Aunt Su's favourite colours. This is the one. I pull it out from the shelf and stare at the cover. There's a girl dressed in a low-cut peasant top standing in front of a long-haired guy in a half-ripped tie-dyed shirt who looks like he wants to eat her for lunch. It's called *Summer of Love*. This one must be from her hippie romance period — I've heard Mom mention these books a few times. It was her best-known series.

Every writer is a reader first.

I flip it open and scan the first page.

That summer changed everything. For me. For Jason. For the entire world. That day I brought home Sergeant Pepper's *and put it on the record player. I could tell from the cover it was going to be great. But what came out of that speaker was like a message blasting across the universe. I shook when I heard it. Nothing was ever going to be the same again.*

No sleepy feelings. But Aunt Su's words feel good. Like a layer of Vaseline smoothing over my injured insides. I close the book with a soft slap and sneak it into the pocket of my hoodie. Why shouldn't I take it home to read? It's not technically wrong, is it? These books *do* belong to me now. Mr. Duffy said so.

By the time I get home, the sky is just beginning to get light. Mom's car is nowhere to be seen and the front door is locked. Inside, there's a note waiting for me on the kitchen table.

Lily,

Didn't want to wake you, but I've left for an early meeting — see you after school.

There are waffles in the freezer for your breakfast. I'd like you to take a break from cereal.

And there's a message for you on the answering machine. Somebody named Emma's inviting you to a party.

???

Mom

Emma? A party? Why on earth is she inviting me? A tornado of irritation touches down in my frontal lobe. With a scowl, I press the glowing red button on the ancient answering machine to hear what she has to say.

"Hey, Lily. It's Emma. Call me back as soon as you can. I just found out there's going —"

My finger stabs the "erase" button, killing the message mid-sentence.

Ça craint!

What's going on here? Why the hell has the universe suddenly decided to bequeath me a wannabe friend?

TEN

Emma Swartz is standing right beside my locker the next morning at school. It almost looks like she's waiting for me. I slow my steps to a crawl, just in case. As soon as she spots me coming down the hall, she rises up on her tiptoes and waves me over. My feet come to a dead stop as my brain buzzes with questions.

What does she think she's doing there? Why is she hounding me? Can I get a restraining order or something?

I wait for a few seconds to see if she'll leave. But when she drops her backpack and smiles at me, I know I'm going to have to go through with it. I trudge up to my locker and start dialling the combination.

7 ...

"Hey, Lily!" Emma chirps.

"Hey."

13 ...

"Did you get my message last night?"

"Nope."

25 ...

"Okay ... Well, Todd Nelson's parents are going away for the weekend and he's having a party tomorrow night. Wanna go?"

"Not really."

35 ...

"Come on, Todd's parties are always fun. He's got a pool and everything."

I turn to stare at her like she's just spontaneously combusted in front of me. Do I really look like the pool party type to her? My backpack catapults onto the floor, just missing a collision with her pink pedicured toes by a measly centimetre. "Okay, Emma ... what's going on? Why are you being so nice to me?"

"W-what do you mean?" she says, her smile melting into a pout. "I'm always nice."

I pull down on the lock and yank open my locker door. Emma jumps back just in time to avoid getting hit by the swinging metal. "What I *mean* is that we haven't spoken one word since the day I attacked your Barbies. Don't you remember?"

"Yeah, I remember."

"So, what gives?"

"Nothing. It's just when I saw you on the first day of school, you looked like you needed a friend. And I ... I guess I kind of did, too."

Okay, now she's officially making *no* sense. "What are you talking about?" I demand. "I am *not* looking for a friend. And can I remind you that you *have* one already. A BFF, even."

Everyone at school knows that Emma Swartz and Sarah Rein have been inseparable since ... well, since the day I attacked her Barbies.

She shakes her head. If I didn't know better, I'd swear she was about to cry. "Something went down over the summer and she kind of stopped talking to me." Her voice is so low, I can barely hear it over the din of the crowded hallway. I close my locker with a bang and wait for more.

"Okay, so what was it?"

"We sort of both had a crush on the same guy," she explains, twirling a thin, red ringlet around her finger, "but he ended up liking me better. And Sarah didn't appreciate that."

Why am I not surprised? Such typical high school pettiness. I can't understand why girls act so jealous and bitchy to each other. I mean, aren't we all on the same team, here?

And on the heels of that thought, I feel so much of my irritation with Emma fade away to nothingness. *We're on the same team, after all.*

Le sigh.

I try my best to insert a bit of friendliness into my voice. Believe you me, that's not so easy for a person who's made it her life's mission to push people away. "Sounds like you're better off without her, Emma."

Her smile makes an instant recovery. "Yeah, anyway," she continues, "you looked all broken up over your aunt and ... well, I've never seen *you* turn your back on a friend."

I let out a sarcastic snort. "Yeah, that's because I never had any." *Come on, did I really need to spell it out for her?*

And that makes her smile balloon into a grin. "Dude, you're avoiding my question," she says, poking me in the arm. "Are you coming to Todd's or not? It's probably going to be the last pool party of the year."

"I don't know."

And I really don't. Just between you and me, the whole idea of a party is kind of horrifying for an introvert like me. But there's a little part of me that wants to go and see what it's all about. I mean, it has to be better than staring at the ceiling and waiting to die. Right? And the way things are going, this will probably be the one and only pool party of my adolescence. How can I pass up the chance to at least check it out?

Just at that moment, Party-Boy Nelson walks past us. Emma reaches out and grabs his arm.

"Todd, wait! Help me convince Lily she should come to the party tomorrow night."

Todd turns to look at me, his eyebrows stretching with surprise. I've been in school with Todd since we were both barely out of diapers. But in all these years, the only time we've ever really spoken was when we were partnered up for a seventh grade science project on volcanoes. Todd's parents own Big Bend's only landscape and garden centre and he works there every weekend and school holiday. Gardening must be good exercise, because Todd is like a wall of muscle — the kind of guy who looks like he was born to be an athlete. He's big, broad, and blond. But he's also the least co-ordinated person you've ever seen in your life. He's always dropping his pen, tripping over his own feet, and bumping into walls. So instead of turning to hockey or football like most of the guys our age, Todd turned to books. He's one of the smartest kids in our school. He won a big provincial science competition last June for his project on hybrid plants. Turns out he developed some kind of species of onion that doesn't make your eyes tear up when you cut into it. That got him a lot of attention. He even got driven in a limo to Toronto to accept the award. If people were fonts, Todd would have to be **Courier**: smart, simple, and strong. The muscle-bound brainiac.

Guess that makes him kind of like an oxymoron too.

"Tell her she should come," Emma urges, poking Todd with her pinky finger.

"Yeah, you should definitely come," he says. There's a big, awkward smile slowly spreading across his face. It almost makes me want to smile too.

Almost. But then I remember the day he publicly outed Aunt Su's secret ganja plantation and the urge to smile fades away.

"So, are you coming?" Emma asks again.

"I don't know, maybe," I finally say. My voice has shrunk to a squeak because, out of the blue, my heart's fluttering again.

"Maybe? What does that mean?" she demands. Todd's green eyes are watching me with interest.

"It means what it means. Maybe I'll see you there. I gotta go now."

The fluttering is suddenly a thundering drum roll. Jeepers creepers, it feels like my chest is going to explode. Last thing I want to do is buy the farm here in the dingy halls of Big Bend High. I rush past Emma and Todd, out the front doors of the school, and down the street. This time, I'm not wasting my energy with that useless school nurse. Believe you me. This time, I'm heading straight to Dr. Vermin's office for a *real* diagnosis.

(Okay, okay— really bad name for a doctor, I know. But he's the only one in Big Bend so it's not as if I have a choice).

By the time I get to his office, my heart's galloping like a greyhound. I march right up to the receptionist and put on my best "emergency patient" face.

"Please. I have to see Dr. Vermin right now. It's urgent."

She doesn't even look up from her computer screen.

"And what's the nature of your problem?"

"I think I'm dying here, lady!" I yelp. A startled hush falls over the waiting room. Yeah, yelling in public is an epic breach of village etiquette. But this happens to be an emergency! The receptionist looks up from her screen, her eyes round as frying pans. She gives a slight nod.

"Okay, yes — you can go ahead inside, then."

I stagger in through the open door and collapse onto the crinkly-papered examination table. Dr. V's pen drops to the floor with a clatter.

"Goodness! What seems to be the problem, Lily?"

At first when I tell him about my heart, he looks mildly concerned. But then, after listening to my chest for a few seconds, he just shakes his head and gives me the same old "nothing to worry about" speech as the school nurse did.

"You're perfectly fine, honey," he says. "Heart palpitations are common enough."

I slap a hand over my eyes and let out a frustrated groan. "No, you don't understand! There's nothing common about it. I think my heart's giving out because I — I'm not sleeping."

He sighs as he bends down to scoop up his dropped pen. "That's nothing new, Lily. From what I remember, you've never been a great sleeper —"

"No!" I cut in. "I mean I'm not sleeping *at all*. Seriously, not a wink in eighteen nights. I'm a nocturnal freak of nature."

Right. So there it is. My huge secret revealed. I hold my breath and wait to hear what Dr. V's going to do about it. Will he call my parents and break the bad news for me? Have me air-lifted to the Mayo Clinic for observation? Or, better yet, offer me a miracle cure to get my sleep back?

I hug my arms to my chest and wait.

"Eighteen days?"

I nod weakly. "Nights, actually. I looked it up on the Internet. It's practically unprecedented."

He brings a hand to cover his mouth. But it doesn't work — the chuckle escapes through his fingers. He turns his back to the wall while he tries to compose himself. After a few seconds, he clears his throat and faces me again.

"I see you've inherited your aunt's talent for storytelling," he says, patting me on the shoulder like a pet poodle. "Let me assure you, your heart is not giving out. Now, with your mother's permission, we can discuss the option of prescribing you a mild sleeping pill if you're having a bit of trouble —"

A mild sleeping pill? General MacArthur's permission?
Great, thanks for nothing.

Feeling more hopeless than ever, I hop down from the table and make for the door.

How could I have been dumb enough to put my trust in a guy named Vermin?

Maybe it's my imagination, but I swear I can still hear him chuckling as I stomp out of the waiting room and into the street.

ELEVEN

It doesn't take me long to get ready. Since I have no idea what to wear to a pool party (aside from a bathing suit, which is *not* going to happen), I just throw on an old pair of comfy jeans and my favourite red sweatshirt. Once it's good and dark out and I've checked to make sure General MacArthur is asleep, I slip on some running shoes and hop out my window.

It's the most beautiful kind of September night. The air is fresh but not cold. And the moon is full and shining golden against the black sky. It looks so big, I feel like I can reach out and take it into my hands. "Hey, buddy," I whisper, giving a little wave like it's an old friend who's come out to play.

I walk for a while down the main road toward Todd's house. The strip is mostly deserted, except for a car full of kids that passes me at top speed, haemorrhaging music from every open window. Probably on their way to Todd's too. The thought of being in the same place as them makes my stomach roll, but I keep going.

I was totally planning on heading straight to the party. Believe you me. I really was. Maybe it's because I'm so nervous, but my feet seem to have other ideas, and the next thing I know, I'm standing in front of McCool Fries, staring down the silver speaker. It hisses at me like a cornered animal. And then for the freakiest of seconds, it really *is* a cornered animal — a hulking grey panther, bristling and snarling at me like it's telling me to back off. A scream rises in my throat as every muscle in my body jumps to high alert. But a moment later, the panther's a speaker again. Just like that. I swallow the scream and shake my head, trying to clear my racing thoughts. *What was that? Man, my brain must be playing serious tricks on me. A panther? Where did that come from? What am I even doing here, anyway?* Closing my eyes, I let my mind slide down the list of possible answers to that question:

Possibility #1 — Party procrastination.
Possibility #2 — Rude Dude confrontation.
Possibility #3 — Sudden adolescent hormonal urge to see the gorgeous jerk again.
Possibility #4 — Good old-fashioned case of the munchies.

That last possibility makes my stomach holler. My eyes flip back open. Yeah, come to think of it, a chocolate McCool's ice cream bar would hit the spot about now. And Ben does owe me after that icky french fry situation from last time. Maybe I can wrangle an explanation about why he slapped away my help in Ms. Pinski's class.

I walk over and peer through the window, ready to wake him up from his nap. But I almost stop breathing when I see him. And not just because of his looks this time. Ben is sitting straight up in his seat with his jacket on — like he's been waiting for me to appear. The black leather jacket from before is gone. In its place is a thin, faded denim jacket that looks like it's been through about a bazillion wash cycles. The room is neat as nerds and, unlike last time, there's no iPod or half-read novel in sight. Before I have a chance to blink, he slides the window open a thin crack and holds up a finger.

"Wait there — don't move."

And then with a slam of the window, he's gone.

What the ...

Moments later, the red door swings open and Ben is standing beside me. He's holding two McCool bars in his hand. "Let's get out of here. I'm dying of claustrophobia."

Is he serious? I glance back at the crappy little cubicle that suddenly looks so sad and empty without him. "But you can't leave it unattended. What if there's a customer?"

He presses a hand to my back and pushes me along. I almost trip over my feet trying to keep up with his long strides. "There *are* no customers, don't you get it? That's why I took this bogus shift. So I wouldn't have to actually do anything." He rips open the wrapper and hands me one of the ice cream bars. "Come on, let's go."

Chocolate. *How did he know?*

"Okay. Thanks."

So we walk along the lakefront pier toward the end of the strip, licking our ice creams and listening to the waves slap up against the sand. The giant moon has lit up a squiggly path on the surface of the water. I have to hold back the urge to jump in the lake and see where it'll lead me.

But to tell you the truth, it's even harder to hold back the urge to attack Ben with a million questions. I want to ask him why he was so rude to me at school. I want to find out who the initials on that ring belong to. I want to ask him why he wouldn't take my help. And why he works in a drive-thru but owns all kinds of expensive things. I want to ask him why he moved here from Toronto. With very few exceptions, people move *away* from Big Bend. They don't move *into* it.

All of these questions are circling around in my head. But I chicken out and don't ask him anything. I guess I'm too nervous.

Let's face it, silence is so much easier than a battle of words. Ben must be feeling the same because neither one of us says anything for a long stretch of time. Which is weird because usually most people feel the need to fill the awkward silence that inevitably goes along with my company. But Ben doesn't seem to mind it. Maybe he's kind of introverted too. I like that thought.

After a while, he turns to me and asks, "So, what time do you have to be home tonight?"

I can feel my cheeks get warm. Hopefully it's too dark for him to notice. "No time. I'm, um, actually going to a party." *God, why do I feel so embarrassed admitting it?*

His eyes amble over my outfit, but he doesn't say anything. A twinge of nerves jabs at my insides. *Are my clothes all wrong? Why do I even care?*

"Want to come with me? It's at Todd Nelson's house. I hear he has a pool." The words are out of my mouth before I can stop them. *Holy crap! Did I really just ask Ben Matthews out on a date?* Suddenly, my underarms start to feel all prickly and hot with nerves. *Dear God, please don't let me get sweat rings under my pits! Why did I do that? He's going to say no. Of course, he's going to say no.*

And he does. But not before laughing first.

"No. Thanks, anyway."

It feels like a punch in the stomach. But I do my best to cover up my disappointment. "Well, I kind of have to make an appearance," I say, struggling to keep my voice casual. "I promised someone I'd be there. So ..."

Ben stops walking and points at my arm. "You're dripping."

Oh God! My pits? Horrified, I look down at myself. I can't tell you how relieved I am to see that it's the ice cream bar melting and not me. Sending out a silent thank you to the universe, I lean over and lap up the long strings of chocolate before they can fall on my shoes. An utterly non-dainty and un-flowerlike slurp escapes my mouth. *Great! Why can't I eat ice cream with a bit of dignity, instead of coming off looking like a messy preschooler? Why can't I ask a guy to a party without getting laughed at? Why is everything about me so wrong on so many levels?*

When I'm done cleaning up the drips, I glance over at Ben. He's finishing off his ice cream bar (neatly, of course) and smiling at me. Probably holding back another laugh. I want to pound him. But instead, I hurl the remainder of my ice cream bar in a nearby garbage container and do what I can to change the subject.

"So, you sure you're not going to get in trouble for ditching McCool's?"

He shrugs. "Trust me, they'll never know I'm gone." Then he smiles and points to a stretch of sand up ahead. "Let's go sit on the beach for a bit."

I look around and see that we've reached the Docks — the area of our village that got its name from the armada of sailboats anchored here during the tourist season. This part of the lakefront is like a national park around here — big open space, soft white sand, sun-bleached picnic tables, and a lake that might as well be an ocean for as far as it stretches toward the horizon. The Docks is the prettiest spot in all of Big Bend. And also the crowdiest. I practically lived on this beach when I was a little kid, playing in the sand and splashing in the water. Now that I'm older, I prefer to come here alone in the early hours of the morning to watch the boats bouncing on the waves and the fishermen bringing in the morning catch. From a distance, of course. As soon as the beach starts to get busy, I skedaddle.

And does it ever get busy around here in the summer. Pretty much every kid in my school works a summer job in the tourist trade. From manning Beachy Keen (our annoyingly adorably named beach shop), to lifeguarding, to day-camp counselling, to waitressing at the Spotted Dick. According to my mom, they all love it. And, according to my mom, I'm the only teenager within a hundred-kilometre radius to opt out of all the summertime fun. Plus, according to my mom (if you still care enough to listen to her ramblings at this point), the definition of summertime fun includes the following: parties, bonfires on the beach, suntanning, and easy, breezy no-strings-attached teenage flings.

But alas, General MacArthur's not-even-halfway-normal, forever-a-disappointment, oxymoronically named, and permanently introverted daughter avoids the tourist crowd scene like the plague. Large groups of fun-seeking, rich, big-city people are about my least favourite things on the planet. And I'm definitely not looking to sunbathe. Unlike the majority of Big Benders, Dad's Sri Lankan roots have blessed me with naturally tanned skin. So instead, I've chosen to spend my summers helping out with the filing system at Dad's office, working on my writing, and hanging out at Aunt Su's cottage. As you can imagine, all of those things give General MacArthur the bonkers.

Good times!

As soon as we find a spot to sit, Ben kicks off his sneakers and digs his feet into the sand. After surviving the near-armpit-disaster, I'm not about to take my shoes off and risk a bad case of smelly-foot-trauma. So I just kneel on the beach and tuck my feet under my butt. The air is definitely cooler here. And breezier, too. I shiver under my bulky sweatshirt, but Ben doesn't seem to notice. He's too busy staring up at the moon.

"It's full tonight. Did you notice?"

The corners of my lips twitch with amusement. *Did he just ask me if I noticed the moon?*

"Yeah, I did."

Another stretch of silence. I listen to the breeze over the water. It sounds like a little kid learning how to whistle.

"You know, when I was really young I used to think my dad lived up there," Ben says after a while.

I turn to look at him. "You did?"

"Yeah, he worked so hard that he was never around. Well, except for Sundays and during our yearly vacation. I used to dream about him quitting his job so he could be there to do the stuff I knew all my friends' dads did. You know ... tuck me in to bed at night, read me stories, take me to McDonald's, drive me to hockey practice. Whenever I'd ask my mother when he was coming home, she'd always say he'd be back late at night — after I was sleeping and the moon was out. I guess somehow I turned that around in my head and imagined that he lived on the moon."

It's the first time he's ever told me something so personal. I watch his expression carefully, hoping it'll tell me even more. But his face stays as blank as a fresh sheet of paper. Suddenly, a picture of a much smaller Ben pops into my head. A little boy sitting alone and slump-shouldered in front of a window, watching and waiting for the day when his father's car would finally pull up in the driveway.

"So sad," I hear myself mumble, then bite my lip and glance at Ben's face to see if he heard. It's one of those thoughts you don't really mean for anyone else to hear but somehow just kind of slips out.

I don't know if Ben heard me or not, because his face still isn't giving anything away. He shrugs. "Now my dad spends every minute of every day at home — something I only dreamed about as a kid. Goes to show ... you gotta be careful what you wish for." And with that, he points a finger toward the sky and abruptly changes the subject. "Look at that, you can totally make out the moon's surface tonight. It sort of looks like a big bruised-up cantaloupe."

I bristle. "It does not."

"Yes, it does. Look again."

I purposely look away. This is just too much. "Sorry, but I don't see cantaloupe. And anyway, scientifically speaking, the moon's really more like a massive, volcanic garden of deep craters and unfulfilled seas." My words are quick and snappy. Ben notices.

"Why are you getting angry? I'm just being honest."

Why am I getting angry? Calling something a banged-up piece of fruit isn't exactly an insult. Maybe I'm being too defensive. This lack of sleep must be making me cranky. And after all, Ben's entitled to his honesty. A feathery breeze blows in from the lake, bringing the aroma of a giant spring rain puddle with it. I fill my lungs up with the smell and let it out slowly. *Honesty.* Ben's right. This is good. And quite possibly a quick shortcut to getting some answers out of him. Deleting all traces of snap from my voice, I angle my body a bit more toward him and say:

"Know what? I like the honesty thing. The moon's not holding anything back tonight. Let's do the same."

His eyebrows shoot up. "What do you mean?"

"We'll ask each other questions. Anything goes. But only the truth, okay?"

I hold my breath and wait for Ben's answer. Will he go for it? His face looks like a beautiful question mark. After a second, the punctuation disappears and he gives a short, little nod. "Okay. But you go first."

I let the breath out. A blizzard of questions falls down around me. Which one to ask first? *Want to tell me why you act like such a jerk all the time?* immediately springs to mind. But that seems a bit too abrasive. Even for me. *Who's SB and why do you wear her ring around your neck? Are you a writer like me? Can I read some of your stuff someday?* But those ones feel a bit too personal to start off with. So instead, I ask this:

"Why did you move here, anyway? If you don't mind me asking? I mean, isn't Toronto supposed to be 'all that'?"

He flops back on the sand and closes his eyes. "You don't want to know. It's a really long story."

Yup. Witness protection program. No doubt in my mind. "Okay, how about you tell me the short version. I've got time." I take a deep breath and steel myself for the gritty truth about what he'd witnessed. *Homicide ... gang activity ... terrorism ... kidnapping?* My brain whirls with big-city criminal possibilities.

After a few seconds, Ben starts talking. His eyes are still squeezed tight like a couple of raisins.

"My family's had a cottage here for years. We've been coming up every summer since I can remember. This year, Dad decided he'd had it with city life and moved us here permanently."

"So it's just the two of you?"

"Yup."

"Where's your mom?"

"Vancouver with her new boyfriend."

Ouch.

"Why don't you live with her?"

"She doesn't want me there."

I wait for him to say more. But he doesn't. He's holding stuff back. I can feel the weight of his secrets crowding the air around us.

"So that's it?" I press.

"You asked for the short version, didn't you?" He looks at me and the raisins turn back into eyes. So dark and blue, the huge body of water in front of me fades away into nothingness.

"Okay, how much for the longer version?"

He doesn't even crack a smile at that. Covering up my disappointment, I slash *witness protection program* off my mental list and move on to the next question. "So you're a writer?"

"Me? Nope."

That throws me for a bit of a loop. "But Pecker said you were the editor of your school paper last year."

Ben waves his hand like he's swatting an invisible fly. "That was just something I did to look good. Same thing with the student council and Junior Achievement. The top schools are pretty competitive and extracurriculars look good on an application, you know?"

"Top schools? You mean universities?"

"Yup."

And then he lets out this strange, snorty kind of laugh that sounds about the farthest thing away from jovial you could imagine. What does that mean? And why is this guy so hard to figure out? I scramble for another question.

"All right. And so, why did you take the graveyard shift at McCool Fries? It's not exactly a job that's going to stand out on your university application. And you don't look like you need the money."

He grunts. "I don't?"

"No. Definitely not. And even if you did, aren't there better jobs around?"

"Dad thought it would be character building to get a job." Ben hooks his fingers around the words "character building" to make it clear it isn't his lame choice of expression. "I saw an ad for the overnight shift at McCool's. The pay was good. It looked easy and, well, since we're being honest, anonymous."

Anonymous. Yeah, that's something I can totally understand.

"And it *has* been pretty much anonymous ... except for you." That kind of sounded like an accusation. But, strangely, his face doesn't look the slightest bit angry. And his eyes are pressing down into mine. Hard. But gentle at the same time. Where to look? What to think? All I know for sure is that my cheeks are starting to get warm again. And I definitely don't want him asking for an honest answer about that! So I point my eyes down, dig my fingers into the sand, and look for pebbles. The silence that follows is a relief.

A minute passes. I can hear a gust of wind blowing toward us across the lake. When it reaches my face, it's surprisingly cold — like a glass of ice water over my head. I shiver and pull my knees up to my chest. A moment later, something soft and warm falls over my shoulders.

What the ...

I turn to see Ben's jean jacket covering me like a blanket. It smells like watermelon shampoo and french fries. My eyes jump to his face. His head is bent over and he's studying the sand at his feet like it's one of those optical illusion puzzles. Under the jacket, he's wearing an old black T-shirt that's faded down to grey from too many washings. And the big expensive watch I'd noticed the first time we met seems to have mysteriously disappeared from his wrist. In its place is a black plastic digital D'watch — on sale for half price at the Big Bend dollar store last week.

"You were looking cold, so ..." Ben's voice trails off into silence.

The jacket is still warm from his body. More than anything, I want to slip my arms through the sleeves, take it home, and tuck it under my pillow. More than anything, I want to throw it back in his face and tell him I don't need his stupid jacket. *What to do, what to do ...*

He starts speaking before I can decide.

"So ... I think it's your turn now."

My turn? So soon? The soft sand goes suddenly lumpy in my hands.

"Okay, what do you want to know?"

A smile inchworms across his lips. "Well, for starters, what are you doing wandering around at all hours of the night? Don't you sleep?"

Sleep. Just the sound of it sends my stomach spinning in circles.

Deep breath in. "That's definitely a longer story than yours."

"Try me."

I lean back on the sand and stare up at the sky. The truth swells painfully against my lips. It would be such a relief to talk about it with someone. But what if Ben has the same reaction as Dr. Vermin? What if he laughs? I lower my eyes and sneak a peek at him through my eyelashes. There's a trace of a frown on his face, like he's worried about what my answer will be. *You should be worried, buddy.* My eyes float back up to the sky. I wonder if that big, bold moon is giving me an extra dose of courage tonight, 'cause a second later I actually come out and confess the truth to Ben. Well, part of it anyway.

"No, I don't sleep. Ever since my aunt died, I can't. Like, not even a little bit." The words scrape my throat raw on the way out.

Long pause.

"Sucks about your aunt," he says.

Deep breath out. "Yeah, thanks."

Another pause. Another chilly gust from the lake. I slip my arms through Ben's long sleeves.

"But really, how do you know for sure?"

"What? That she's dead?"

"No. How do you know you're not sleeping?"

"What do mean?"

"I mean, how can you be sure? Are you video recording yourself?"

I twist my neck around to stare at him. "What do you mean? How does anybody know if they're not sleeping?"

"Easy. Sometimes you can be so tired, you can just fall asleep without realizing it so then you think you're awake. It happens to me all the time. Especially in trig, for some reason."

I sit straight up. A thin trickle of sand runs down the back of my shirt into the crack of my jeans. Something about what he said is making my brain twitch. There was something on that National Sleep Research Project website about this. Something about how people can fall asleep with their eyes open and not even know it. But I would know if I fell asleep. I'm sure I would.

Wouldn't I?

"I think there's even a name for it," Ben continues. "Micro-sleeping, or something like that."

My throat tightens with irritation. "Yeah, well, that's not what's happening to me," I snap back. "I'm not micro-sleeping. I'm not sleeping *at all*. Which means I'm probably ..." I have to squeeze my lips shut to keep the word *dying* from falling out of my mouth.

Shadows fall over Ben's face as a cloud passes over the moon. "It means you're probably *what*?" he asks.

I swallow hard and twist my finger inside the hole in the left knee of my jeans. "I-it means I'm probably a complete freak of nature," I say, doing my best to change the subject. Honesty pact or not, I'm not ready to share the other part of my truth with him yet. Especially when he's so obviously holding back secrets of his own.

"A freak of nature?" he repeats.

"Yeah."

I lift my eyes back to Ben's face. His eyebrows are arched up into a pair of perfect crescents. "That sounds pretty harsh."

Is that a laugh hiding behind his words? Or am I just totally paranoid?

"It *is* harsh, for your information. I haven't slept in over eighteen days. Do you have any idea how unprecedented that is? It's, like, completely out of the realm of documented human experience."

I hold my breath as the words fill the space between us. Is he going to read between the lines and figure out the rest of the awful truth? That I'm on the fast track to an early death?

I wait. Ben's eyes drop down to my mouth. "And even worse, your face is covered in chocolate." Leaning over me, he reaches a hand out and wipes at a spot on my cheek right near my lips. My skin burns in the place where he touches it ... like his fingers are mini blowtorches. Recoiling back, I reach up to cover them before he can see me turn red.

"So, you're saying you don't believe me about not sleeping?" I demand.

He actually has the nerve to smirk. "It's a bit far-fetched."

I pound a frustrated fist into the sand. "Ben, I'm telling the truth."

"Okay, relax." He holds up his hands in mock surrender. "Fine. You're a total freak of nature, all right? You don't have to get so upset about it."

But I don't think he really believes me. Just like that quack Dr. Vermin. And all of a sudden, our little honesty pact is completely off the table.

"I'm not upset at all," I say. *Yes, I am.* "You can believe whatever you want." *You big, dumb, jerk.* "It's late. I guess I'm just cranky and overtired." *And dying a torturously slow death.*

I pull my arms tight around me and drop my gaze back down to my jeans. Suddenly I'm regretting this whole honesty thing. Tears burn at my eyes but I blink them away before they can leak out. Ben is still watching me. I can feel it. But I don't want him seeing me like this.

Out of the corner of my eye, I see him check his D'watch. Then he lets out a noise that sounds kind of like a half groan blendered with a half growl. "Man, I hate myself for saying this, but I better get back to the drive-thru." He yawns and pulls himself to his feet. "So, you still going to that party?"

Nod.

"Come on, I'll walk you there if you want." He reaches a hand down to help me up. His blowtorch fingers waggle in front of my face. I ignore them and stand up on my own. Maybe it's stubbornness, but I don't want his help.

Just his jacket.

"You don't have to walk me," I say, clapping the sand off the back of my jeans. "I can make it there on my own."

He laughs again and tilts his head up to the sky. "Are you sure about that? The lunatics will be out tonight in droves."

Lunatics? Even through the dark, he must see the confusion in my eyes.

"Clearly you're not as good with languages as you are with math."

Obviously, he hasn't heard me swear yet. Actually, I take enriched classes in French and English Lit. Confession time: I'm kind of a browner with words too. But I don't need to prove myself to Ben Matthews. Instead, I pull off a sneaker and let a stream of sand pour out. "I have no idea what you're talking about," I say, forcing my voice to sound just as bored as his.

"*Lunatic* comes from the word *lune*. You know, French for *moon*? Haven't you heard the theory that crime rates skyrocket when there's a full moon? Something about the pull of gravity on our bodies."

First the cantaloupe crack and now this? I finish emptying the other sneaker and cross my arms in front of me like a shield. Okay, I'm fully aware how weird this is going to sound, but I'm feeling bizarrely possessive about the moon—like nobody better be disrespecting it around me. "I'll take my chances. Thanks anyway."

"Still, I'll walk you there just in case. You village people are all way too trusting for your own good. I mean, you guys don't even lock your doors around here."

"Yeah, and you city people are all too arrogant for your own good," I growl back. He stares at me in surprise. Lifting my chin, I hold his gaze until he looks away. I hear him mumble a few words under his breath. It sounds something like, "Well, I'm not a city person anymore."

Right. So maybe it's time to start trusting people a little bit more. I don't actually say that last part. But I wish I had.

He starts walking back toward the main strip. "So what street is this party on?"

"Birch."

My voice is gruff and raw — like one of Mom's double-sided emery boards. I follow a couple of steps behind. Silence surrounds us again — a welcome relief. Then, after about five minutes, Ben slows his strides so we're walking side by side.

"Have you tried warm milk?"

I look at him in shock. A sleeping cure? *Does that mean he believes me now?*

"Y-yeah, of course I have."

"What about counting sheep?"

I nod. "Fields of 'em."

He's quiet for a minute. And then this:

"Relaxing thoughts?"

"Yup."

"Breathing exercises?"

I let out an exhausted sigh. "Ben, believe me, I've tried every-thing humanly possible to get to sleep. But nothing works. It's like I'm fighting a losing battle."

He doesn't reply to that. We continue the rest of the way to Birch Street in silence. Ben walks me to Todd's house, all the way to the top of the driveway. The Nelsons' house is huge, which makes me think the garden and landscape business must be one of the only things thriving in this wrecked economy. The party has spilled outside. It's a pretty messed-up scene. The front yard is littered with kids — some are smoking dope, some making out, some puking in the bushes, and a few are completely passed out on the grass. The entire house is pulsing with music. Lucky for Todd, his property is big. I know if there were any neighbours within earshot, the RCMP would be all over this place.

"Sure you want to go in there?" Ben asks.

Barely perceptible nod.

"It looks pretty wild." He points in the general direction of a guy staggering across the lawn and chugging back a bottle of beer. I notice Ben's eyes go dark and his lips press together into a hard line. Whoa, if I didn't know better, I'd think he was actually worried about me.

"I'll be fine. Someone's waiting for me in there. I better go."

Ben sighs. "Okay, have fun. See you at school." And with that, he turns and walks away.

Why is my stomach suddenly hurting to see him leave? I follow him a couple of steps down the driveway. "Ben! Wait ... Why don't you come in for a minute? Have a drink or something?"

He shakes his head and holds a hand up to stop me. "No, really, thanks. It's not my scene."

That surprises me. A lot. I make a mental note to scratch *Mafioso son of a drug dealer* off the list too. If he really was a drug dealer, for sure he'd say yes to the party. I mean, isn't that the best kind of place to hook new customers? I peer at him as he walks off down the driveway. This guy is turning out to be more of a mystery than I bargained for.

"Okay ... see you," I call out. But I don't think he hears me. I watch as he slowly fades into the darkness, following the path of the moon.

TWELVE

Pretty much everyone at Todd's party is smashed. Believe you me. Even the dog looks stoned from all the second-hand pot smoke in the air. I push my way through the crowd. Where's Emma? Not in the hallway. Not in the living room. How 'bout the kitchen? Someone hands me a glass as I walk through the doorway. I have no idea what it is, but it looks red and icy and it tastes sweet. I drink it down in a couple of gulps. And then someone hands me another. I drink that too. And then another.

What the hell. Maybe *this* is what I need to fall asleep.

Problem is, when you don't even weigh a hundred pounds with your snow boots on, it doesn't take more than one or two drinks to put you over the edge. After the third, Todd's party loses any and all charm for me. After only ten minutes, the smell of smoke is turning my stomach. And the reek of alcohol is hanging in the air like a smelly damp cloud. Plus, the music is so loud I can feel my skull throb. Giving up on finding Emma, I slide open the screen door and wander outside to the backyard. Todd's dog follows me outside, clearly happy to get into the fresh air. A few couples are in the swimming pool, fooling around in the water. I pretend they're large fish and keep walking. Jeepers creepers, what is it about water that makes people so horny?

The air is better out here. I take some deep breaths. My head is spinning in slow-moving circles. It's kind of nice, actually. I drop down onto one of the lime green lounge chairs that surround the pool. I close my eyes and the spinning gets a bit faster. Like I'm riding one of those teacup rides Dad used to take me on at the annual Canada Day fair. I lean my head back on the lime green cushion, curl onto my side, and try my best to enjoy it. Maybe sleep is finally on the way. My thoughts drift back to Ben and the spinning goes faster still.

Suddenly, I feel a tapping on my shoulder. My eyes open to a narrow squint. Bleary Emma is standing above me hugging a beer, her eyes glassy like lake water. Beside her is Bleary Todd — owner of this house of wrecked kids.

"Hey, s'up?" I mumble. My words sound like they're coming from the other side of the yard. Wild. "I've been looking for you, Emma."

She has a freckled arm wrapped around Todd's shoulder. *Just like a polka-dot scarf*, I hear a little voice that doesn't sound entirely unlike Aunt Su's say in my head. *Har-har.*

"Just here to cash in on a little bet," Emma says, her words running into each other like a melting cherry slushie. "Todd didn't believe me when I told him you were here. When I said you were out in the backyard, he thought I was yanking his chain. Bet me five bucks."

As soon as that last word is past her lips, she lets out a loud hiccup and a giggle. Todd laughs too. "Hey, Lily, did you bring any party favours from your aunt's garden?" He's smiling at me, probably too drunk to realize how hurtful that comment is. Pulling the bottle of beer out of Emma's hands, he tilts his head back and drains it dry. My stomach lurches at the sight. All I want to do is close my eyes and get back to my spinny teacup ride.

"So you see?" Emma turns and punches him in the ribs. "She's here like I said she was. Now pay up, smartass!"

I watch as Bleary Todd fishes a fiver out of his pocket and slaps it into Bleary Emma's hand. My eyelids begin to feel like there are lead weights attached to them. Emma disentangles herself from Todd's arm and holds up the bill in triumph.

"Hey, Lily, I'll treat you to some fries. Maybe at the drive-thru later tonight?"

Her voice rises to a squeal on the words *drive-thru*. With a wink, she turns around and stumbles back towards the house. As soon as we're alone, Todd sits down on the end of the lounge in the big empty space where my short legs can't reach. He shoots me a sheepish, little-boy smile. "Sorry about that whole bet thing. I just didn't believe it when she said you were here tonight. I'm pretty sure I've never seen you out at any party before."

"Yeah, I usually try to avoid scenes like this."

Todd's smile widens as he leans back on his elbows. *Wow, he has nice teeth.*

"Why? Are you shy or something?"

There's that word again. "No," I snap, maybe a little too harshly. "Not at all. Just highly selective about the company I keep."

Todd sits up straight and I can see his pale eyebrows scrunch together with hurt. "So why'd you bother coming here tonight if we're all so beneath you?"

I roll my eyes at my own stupidity. Now can you see why I avoid people? I always end up saying the wrong thing and coming off like a bitch. I feel bad. I reach for his hand to apologize. Problem is at that moment, Bleary Todd is sporting four hands (and two heads). Trying to focus my eyes as much as possible, I take a shot in the dark and somehow manage to choose the one of the hands that isn't a drunken mirage.

"No, that's not what I meant. I'm actually glad I came here tonight. I've always been curious to, you know, see what these things are all about."

I can tell he likes my answer because the scrunch in his forehead smoothes right out. We stare at each other like that for a few seconds. Todd is actually pretty good looking. And I'm not just thinking that because I'm smashed. Why have I never noticed him before? Like, *really* noticed him? And, more to the point, why does he suddenly seem to be noticing me?

That's when one of the couples who were making out in the pool climb up the side and throw their dripping selves down onto the lime green lounge chair beside us. And then they start flopping around like two giant fish out of water. Suddenly the view is all sliding tongues, speeding hands, and twisting torsos. It's like a scene right out of Aunt Su's romance novels — without the luxury of being able to close the book and toss it onto the floor. Yeah, holding Todd's hand and watching these two make out right beside us is quite possibly one of the more awkward moments I've ever had to endure. Then the girl lets out a little moan and the whole thing officially takes the gold medal for cringe-worthiness.

Forgetting all about Todd for a minute, I close my eyes so I don't have to watch the X-rated scene going on beside me. But the slurpy sound of their lips sucking on each other is impossible to escape. I'm just about to get up and run away when I feel a hand gliding around the back of my neck. Todd must have taken my closed eyes as some kind of an invitation because the next thing I know, his mouth is on mine. My eyes pop open in shock. For a few seconds, I can't even move. His lips are kind of chapped and his breath smells like beer and weed. After I get over my initial impulse to smack him away, I decide to let him push his tongue into my mouth. I mean, what the hell; I'm dying anyway, right?

Okay, confession time again. This is kind of my first kiss. Yup, that kiss you're destined to remember forever because it's the first *real* one. Except I'm not sure I want to be remembering it forever. Even if my forever *is* only a few more days. For starters, it's a whole lot messier than I imagined it would be. When you watch people making out in the movies or on TV, it all seems so perfect and neat. And this is all wet and kind of squishy — like there's an oversized goldfish swimming around in my mouth. Don't get me wrong, I want to enjoy it. The aching hole inside me that Aunt Su left needs to be filled and this seems like a decent way to do it. So, I let Todd kiss me for a while. I even kiss him back. After a few minutes, he starts to pick up speed. I can hear his breath panting against my face and I know he's getting way more excited about this than I am. As much as I want to like the whole first-kiss thing, it just isn't happening for me. Cute as Todd is, he's kind of slobbery and his tongue sweeping through my mouth is about as exciting as a dental cleaning. When I feel his hands climb up under my shirt and start fumbling with the back of my bra, I decide to put the brakes on. For God's sake, a klutz like Todd could work for an hour with those tiny little clasps and not get anywhere. Just the thought of it smashes any infinitesimal chance at the romance I'm trying to force myself into feeling.

I'm so over it.

My first kiss, sealed forever in a flush of beer-flavoured spit. *This* is what all the fuss is about? Call me crazy, but I think dying alone while counting the tiny stucco bumps on my bedroom ceiling is better than this. See what a freak of nature I am? The only teenager in the world who doesn't like to party, get wasted, and have casual sex.

Pushing him off me with one hand, I drag the other over my mouth to wipe away the trail of his spit on my lips. "Stop, Todd," I say, swinging my legs off the lounge. "I'm tired. I want to go home now."

He looks so disappointed — like a kid whose ice cream cone just fell over into the sand. "Why?" he whines. "I thought we were just getting started."

Sheesh! Is this how guys get their way with girls? By handing out guilt trips?

"Sorry, I ... I just gotta go."

"Wait!"

Too late. I jump up and start walking away before he can say anything else. My head is still spinning, but I manage to get away without falling over.

Walking home is a balancing act, but I make it in one piece. And the entire time, all I can think about is Ben. And the stack of secrets he seems to be working so hard to hide.

And how goddamned much I wish it had been him kissing me tonight instead of Todd.

THIRTEEN

I know something is wrong the second I walk through the front door. All the lights are on and the house is practically humming with nervous expectation. And when I hear an all-too-familiar tapping noise coming from the kitchen, I brace myself for the inevitable confrontation.

General MacArthur is awake. And, by the sound of it, none too happy.

Just great.

Trying my best to act as sober as possible, I walk slowly and steadily down the hall and into the fire. She's waiting for me — sitting at the round, glass table, arms folded defensively over her chest and legs crossed so tightly I think she might actually be about to cut off the blood supply to her toes. Her red slipper is bouncing up and down restlessly, hitting the floor in a frantic drumbeat. And there's a half-eaten, slowly soggifying bowl of Cheerios in front of her.

Crap, how long has she been waiting up?

"Where have you been, Lily?" Her voice is low — practically a growl.

I take a deep breath, hoping the answer won't come out all slurry and drunk. *Take it easy, Lily. Short and simple and she'll never know.*

"Out at a friend's housh ... house."

General MacArthur actually smiles at that. "But you don't have any friends, my dear."

She has me there. I take another deep, sobering breath. "Well, I'm trying to change things up this year. Thought you'd be happy about that."

Now, as you can probably imagine, all those sobering breaths aren't such a smart idea. Because it doesn't take long for the smell of my sins to blow straight over to Mom's nose and rat me out.

"I can smell the alcohol on your breath from here," she says, her thin nose wrinkling. "What have you been drinking?"

Shrug.

"I don't know."

"And is that smoke I smell on you?"

I have no choice but to full-out confess. Trust me, you'd have done the same thing in my shoes. Let's face it, hiding the truth is just going to make it worse. Control freaks like my mother don't handle lies very well — throws their perfect world way off axis.

"Okay, yeah, smoke and alcohol. It was a party. You've heard of those, right?"

She lets out a loud, gusty sigh. "Lily, you're fifteen! Drinking and smoking are illegal at your age! Did you know that?"

"Yeah."

Another sigh. At this rate, she's going to hyperventilate. With any luck, maybe she'll pass out. My left hand rises up behind my back and I secretly cross my fingers.

"In this condition, I just hope you weren't anywhere near the water tonight."

I shake my head, pushing the images of the lake and the pool out of my thoughts. She doesn't have to know the whole truth, does she?

"So, what exactly were you thinking, young lady?"

I shrug to let her know I don't care. To tell you the truth, for the first time in history I'm not really that scared of her. Guess when you're facing imminent death by exhaustion, a yelling mother isn't such a big deal. I mean, really — what can she possibly do to make my life any worse than it is? Demerit points?

"I just knew something was up when you got that phone message from that girl Emma. You know, some parents out there would call the police and let them press charges for a stunt like this. Maybe that would be the best way for you to learn a lesson about responsibility."

WTF? Okay, so prison, on the other hand, is kinda scary. I stare at her closely, trying to figure out if she's serious or not. She stares back at me, her eyes like stones.

"Come on, Mom." My voice is pleading now. "Don't tell me you waited until you were legal to have your first drink."

She doesn't even blink at that. Man! How is it possible that she and Aunt Su were even remotely related?

"*Merde*, Mom —"

"I understand French too, and there's no call for swearing, young lady." She pushes her half-eaten bowl of cereal at me. "Here, eat something."

My stomach flops over at the sight of it.

"No, thanks."

"Eat! It'll help you metabolize that alcohol and save me the trouble of having to clean up the mess of vomit that's surely coming."

I'm about to refuse again when I remember what Dad said about her worrying. Something about how she only pushes food at me when she's freaking out. My thoughts fly back to all those weekend days at the Docks when I was a little kid. She used to follow me into the ocean with food in her hands, pushing me to eat something when all I wanted to do was play in the waves. And all those days when she'd show up after my swimming lessons with a gallon of cookies in her purse. With a sigh, I sink into the nearest chair.

"Can I at least have something that's not soggy?"

She stands up and walks slowly to the cupboards. When she comes back, she's carrying a clean bowl, a spoon, and a Pyrex container filled with strawberries. I pop one in my mouth while General MacArthur fills my bowl with fresh Cheerios.

"I know it's not the first time you've snuck out at night," she says quietly, dropping into the seat beside me. I scoop a spoonful of cereal into my mouth and crunch. Right now, that's the only answer she's gonna get out of me.

"This behaviour isn't at all like you, Lily," she presses. "You haven't been yourself since Su died."

Hey, give the lady a prize! I shovel another spoonful into my mouth.

Her hand lands ever so gently on my back. "How's your sleeping?"

Shrug. "Beachy keen."

Exasperated mom sigh #3.

"So, want to tell me what's going on?"

I shake my head so hard it almost throws the rest of me off balance. If Mom finds out I'm dying a slow death by exhaustion, she'll come up with a drastic way to try and fix it. Like taking me to the hospital and demanding a medically induced coma or something insane like that. No, asking for her help is just asking for more trouble.

She stands up slowly, hands slipping into the pockets of her robe. Her lips are pressed together in a thin pink line. Just watch, this is the part where she loses it. My mother needs control and I'm flat out refusing to pass over the reins. Her nostrils flare with outrage. Okay, here it comes ...

"I don't think you're leaving me much choice here, Lily. My job as your mother is to keep you safe. So I'm grounding you until further notice. There'll be no more sneaking out at night."

Her job as my mother? What, am I just some kind of work assignment? I force myself to swallow a mouthful of mashed-up Cheerios. "Fine. Whatever," I mumble. *Go ahead and try to stop me. I've still got a window, you know.*

As if she's reading my thoughts, Mom slides a perfectly mani- cured finger under my chin and raises my face up 'til I'm forced to meet her gaze.

"Just in case this conversation slips your mind, Lily — I'll be installing a lock on your bedroom window first thing tomorrow. And another one on your bedroom door. To help you remember."

A lock on my bedroom door? *Just like when I was a toddler.* I jerk my chin away. "Fine. Whatever." There's no sense arguing with her when she's like this.

Mom's eyes rake sideways across my body. "And what are you wearing? Did your father get you a new coat?"

Huh? I look down at myself.

Ben's jean jacket.

"It's much too big. Tell him to take it back and get you a smaller size. You're almost sixteen, for goodness' sake. Does that man really think you're still growing?"

I close my eyes and pray for the room to stop spinning. "I don't know …"

· She heaves out an exasperated breath.

"Tell me, have you figured out what to do with those disgusting ashes yet?"

"Oh God, Mom, please don't do this now …"

I can hear the sound of her fingers drumming on the tabletop. "You know, I stopped by her cabin today."

My eyes pop open. Something about her voice is warning me

to be on guard. "Yeah, so?"

Her slipper begins to pick up the frantic beat again (naturally, in perfect time with her tapping fingers). "So, I didn't realize how decrepit that place had become," she continues. "I mean, it's leaning over like it might collapse any moment. And the inside is so musty and damp, I almost choked on the air. I'm afraid to find out what kind of toxic mould is growing behind those walls."

I hold up a hand to make her stop. I think I'm having another one of those palpitations. My heart is fluttering so hard, it feels like there's a hummingbird trapped inside my chest. "You're exaggerating. It's not that bad!"

"Oh, no?" she asks, her voice rising to a near screech. And her slipper is hammering the floor so hard, I'm sure she's going to make a dent. "Well, then how about the marijuana plants growing all over the garden? Did you know about those? Your beloved aunt was practically running a grow-op out there!"

"Mom, don't even …"

"First thing Monday morning, I'm going to speak to Mr. Duffy about having it condemned."

My mouth falls open. "What are you talking about? The garden?"

"Don't be stupid, Lily. I'm talking about the cabin. Every single thing about that place is a hazard. Not to mention illegal."

I feel like my heart is trying to pound its way out of my body. Ignoring my spinning head, I push off from the table and somehow make it up to my feet. "You've got to be joking! You actually want to have her cabin torn down?"

Her head swivels back and forth on her skinny neck. "It's not that I want to, Lily. I have to. Trust me, it should have been done years ago."

Jeepers creepers! I want to shake her by the shoulders and

demand she tell me where she buried her heart. "How can you even suggest this? That cabin was Aunt Su's whole, entire world! Tearing it down would be like ... like having her die all over again!"

"Lily, listen to me ..."

"No!" I squeeze my eyes shut, blocking her out of my sight. I'm so angry, I can't even stand to look at her. "You listen to me for once! That cabin belongs to me now! Do you understand? *Me!* Mr. Duffy even said so! And nobody's going to touch it without my permission!"

Pushing back my chair, I rocket to my feet and bolt out of the kitchen before she can see the expression of complete and utter hatred on my face. I go straight upstairs, slip my arms out of the sleeves, and tuck Ben's jean jacket under my pillow right next to Aunt Su's drawing. The two things the EMS workers are going to find under my lifeless, exhausted body when they come to toe-tag me. The image brings a sickening wave of panic rolling through my stomach. My heart is still galloping like racehorse. But of course, it's "nothing to worry about" — right Dr. V? I glance over at the pomegranate jar sitting on my desk. And then a horrible image of Aunt Su's cabin getting bulldozed to the ground slithers through my thoughts. With a sob, I stagger to the bathroom and heave up a toiletful of Cheerios and tears.

This is day (night) nineteen without sleep.

I'm officially living on borrowed time.

A Short and Very Angry Note from Me

General MacArthur went ahead and did it.

I know ... big surprise, right?

Yup, just like she promised, the locksmith arrived first thing yesterday morning before I was even fully awake. While he was setting up my prison cell, I grabbed the phone, staggered out to the backyard, and called up Mr. Duffy. I didn't even care that it was a weekend. I had to ask him if the General has the right to bulldoze Aunt Su's cabin, since it is, after all, my bequeathing property now. He said no, she doesn't have the right to bulldoze it. Which, as you can imagine, made me feel way better.

For about a nanosecond.

Because then he went on to say something like "not without just cause." When I asked what that meant, he told me if the building doesn't meet provincial safety standards, Mom has the right to report it to the authorities and request that it be condemned. Apparently, she doesn't need permission from the owner (insert my name here) to do that.

That's when the angry, itchy rash began spreading over my insides.

"And what if it's condemned?" I asked Mr. Duffy, "What happens then?"

"Then no person will be allowed within thirty metres of the cabin. And the municipality can order it torn down if necessary."

Ça craint!

I told him to expect a call from my mother first thing the next morning. Believe you me, Mr. Duffy sounded none too pleased about that little tidbit of information. Then I got him to promise me he'll stall the filing process for a few days. Hopefully, that'll give me some time to get the cabin up to standard. I won't let it be condemned. You, my friend, are now an official witness ... because I swear on Aunt Su's pomegranate jar-of-ashes that I will not let my mother get away with this.

All I have to do now is figure out how to stay alive long enough to stop her.

FOURTEEN

September 16th

I've spent every minute of the last two days and nights trying to figure out a way to save Aunt Su's cabin from the heartless, controlling beast that calls herself my mother. Yeah, I was so busy obsessing over it, I almost missed noticing when Ms. Pinski finally caught herself a fly Monday morning. I guess it was only a matter of time — Ben's been struggling to stay awake in our first-period trig class since the first day of school. And I totally saw it coming just seconds before it happened, 'cause he was snoring loud enough to pull my eyes away from the clock above the blackboard, where I'd been watching the remaining seconds of the little cabin's doomed existence tick by. And his head was bobbing up and down like a cork on the waves. I kicked the underside of his chair and poked him between the shoulder blades with my pencil to wake him up. See? That's how nice of a person I can be. But it was too late. I swear, Pinski's voice was squeaking with excitement when she caught him. Like so many math teachers, she has a secret sadistic side.

"I'm sorry, are we keeping you up, Mr. Matthews?"

Ben was slapped with a week's worth of detention. Got off pretty easy, if you ask me. But then, good-looking people always seem to get off easy, don't they?

I catch up to him after class by his locker. "Hey, Ben." He half glances my way but doesn't seem to see me. I crank my voice up a notch, just in case the drone of hallway chatter is drowning out my words. "So, sucks about that detention, huh?"

This time he definitely hears me. "Yeah. It sucks," he says, but he still isn't looking at me and his voice sounds like it's light years away from his answer. Something's wrong.

"Ben?"

His face tilts down toward mine and I watch as his pupils slowly ease into focus. It almost seems as if he's sleepwalking. He looks so tired — like all he wants to do is lie down and rest. And there's something else in his eyes that's never been there before. If I didn't know better, I'd say it was panic. But that doesn't make any kind of sense; why would Ben be freaking out over something as minor as a detention? Forgetting about my own problems, I suddenly find myself consumed with the overwhelming urge to help him. He's like a big puppy in a rainstorm. So completely adorable and so totally pathetic all at once. It's irresistible. I want to wrap my arms around him and give him a hug. But of course, I'm not about to do that. Not with the whole school watching. So instead, I lean against his locker and lower my voice so nobody else can hear.

"Hey, why don't you just tell Pinski about your job at the drive-thru? Maybe if she knew, she'd cut you a bit of slack about the sleeping thing."

He shakes his head. "I don't think that's a good idea."

Well, I'm not going to give up that easily. Believe you me. And yes, I admit it: my stubborn streak is something I inherited from Mom. I poke my finger against the little magnetic mirror stuck to the inside of the open locker beside his. "Look at yourself here, Ben. You can't even keep your eyes open for more than a few minutes. It's like you're a walking zombie."

But he ignores the mirror and me and focuses instead on loading books into his backpack. One at a time ... painfully slowly. Like he's trying to drive me crazy.

God, why is it so much easier to talk to him when we're alone together at night?

And then I have an idea so genius I blurt it out without even thinking it through. "Hey, I know: why don't you let me take a few shifts at McCool Fries for you so you can catch up on some sleep?

I really thought that would make him smile — maybe even show a bit of gratitude for once. After all, I've been trying to save his ass around here since day one. But instead, he just shakes his head so hard it sends the little silver initial ring hanging around his neck swinging from side to side. He grabs the ring and squeezes it for a second before tucking it back inside the collar of his shirt. "Unh-uh. No. I can't let you do that."

"Really, Ben, I don't mind. I want to do it. Let me help you out." I lower my voice another notch. "It's like I told you last weekend, I'm awake all night anyway."

Okay, in hindsight I probably shouldn't have been making offers like that. I mean, I *am* grounded, after all. There's no way Mom is going to unlock my cage and let me go work the grave-yard shift at McCool Fries. But I'm feeling like I have to help him. Like helping him out might make me forget about my own problems with sleep ... and saving Aunt Su's cabin. In the end, it doesn't matter whether I can take the shift or not, because for whatever twisted reason, Ben is determined not to let me help him. Like, *really* determined.

"No!" His voice cuts through me like a blade. It's so loud, I actually jump back with surprise. When he looks up from his books, his eyes are hard again. Just like they were that first night I met him. As if that night we spent at the Docks never even happened. As if every conversation we'd ever had has been rubbed out by a giant eraser and we've gone right back to the starting line.

"But —"

Ben's face goes dark. "I said no! Can't you just drop it?"

He's full out hollering now. For a second, the hallway chatter freezes in mid-air while everyone looks around to see who's getting reamed out. My cheeks flare up with heat as I suddenly feel every pair of eyes zero in on me. I notice Todd Nelson standing a few metres away. His eyes are bouncing between me and Ben and his face is all clenched like a fist. A second later, he starts marching towards us. To his credit, he only stumbles once.

"Are you okay, Lily?"

Oh, spare me. Not the white-knight-coming-to-the-rescue-of-the-damsel-in-distress thing.

"Yes, I'm fine, Todd." I force a half smile so he'll believe me. It doesn't seem to work. He takes a step closer to Ben. "Are you sure this new guy's not bothering you?" he grunts.

I put my hands on his shoulders and give him a gentle push back in the opposite direction. "No, Todd, he's not bothering me. You can go now. He's just way overtired."

Luckily, Todd takes the hint and leaves. But when I turn back around, I see the backside of Ben striding off down the hallway. I sprint to catch up. "Ben, wait," I say, taking his arm. He stops walking and swings around to look at me, eyes flashing with anger. When he speaks, his voice is a growl of warning. "God, Lily! I really wish you wouldn't go around telling everyone about my problems. Didn't I ask you to drop it?"

Okay, this is getting to be too much. All I wanted to do was help.

"I'm sorry ... I-I just ..."

"That's the point! I don't want anyone feeling sorry for me ... especially not you!"

"I-I wasn't feeling sor—"

His palms fly up in front of my face, like a traffic cop trying to stop a speeding car. "I mean it! Just. Leave. Me. Alone!" And then he's marching away down the hall again. This time I let him go. I can feel every nosy eyeball in that hallway watching me, waiting to see what I'm going to do. My eyes fall to the floor and I have to bite my lip to keep from yelling something stupid and hurtful after him.

I'm so angry I don't even notice Emma come up beside me until she puts a hand on my shoulder and gives it a pat. "It's okay, Lily. Don't let Ben get to you. He's been acting like that to everyone since he moved here. You can't take it personally."

I shake her hand off my shoulder and whirl around to face her. My cheeks are still burning with humiliation. "When someone treats me like crap, I can't help taking it personally!" Because I know he's out of earshot by now, I let my anger loose. "Ben Matthews is a total *branleur*!" I yell this at the top of my voice so that every single person in that hallway will hear me and understand exactly how much I hate him. Well, at least every single person who understands French curses. And for the benefit of those who don't, I add this in English: "He's a snob and a half, and he's rude to everyone he meets."

Emma just smiles this strange smile that just makes me angrier than ever. The smile is so big, I can see breakfast scraps stuck in her braces. So big, I can see a few tiny little freckles dotting the pink of her gums. How awesomely weird is that? I'm on the verge of developing a new respect for Emma. And then she blows it by saying what is quite possibly the dumbest thing I've ever heard:

"Funny, I think you guys make a perfect match."

A perfect match? I'm so shocked, I can barely squeak out a simple one word answer. "W-why?"

"Can't you see it?" she continues, enjoying my reaction. "It's so obvious. You two are *exactly* alike."

I feel like I've just been punched in the stomach. "We are *not!*" I hiss, looking around to see if anyone else has heard her. "We are absolutely *nothing* alike! For starters, I'm not rude, arrogant, or a snob."

"Okay, so what are you, then?" Emma asks, folding her arms in front of her chest like a lawyer cross examining a guilty witness. "Why is it that you haven't spoken to anyone in this school since, like, kindergarten?"

My mouth hangs open.

"I'm … I'm just … introverted."

Introverted. The word escapes my lips in a whisper. It's almost as if Aunt Su's warning is ghosting through my brain.

Better get used to a snooty reputation, Lily-girl.

I lean back against the locker and squeeze my eyes shut. *Me and Ben, exactly alike? Really?* And then my shoulders sag with the awful weight of it and I know it's true. *Tabernac.* How could Emma have seen it while I missed it so completely? That's totally why I can't stop thinking about him. We are so completely and utterly alike. The only difference is that I know exactly why I push people away.

What's Ben's excuse?

FIFTEEN

Everything reminds me of Ben these days. It's absolutely, positively, mind-bendingly infuriating! After the big, ugly blow-up at his locker, I've been doing everything in my power to avoid him. I ignore him when we pass in the halls, act like he's invisible when I see him in the cafeteria, and pretend he's the equivalent of absolute zero in trig class. Basically, I've done everything I know how to cut him out of my thoughts. But it's like the more I stay away from thinking about him, the more he takes over my brain. I can't even read a book without picturing his face in my head or hearing his voice in my ears. I've been stuck on the same paragraph of Aunt Su's *Summer of Love* for an hour now.

Jason was one of many. But then, so was I. His face rose out of the crowd like the sun coming up over the horizon. One look and I was gone. Blinded. The crowd blurred into the background as he came toward me.

Merde.

Guess reading a romance novel isn't exactly the best way to forget a guy. With a sigh, I let the book fall into my lap and turn my face toward the window. There's another half moon tonight. I watch it with squinty eyes, trying to make out the part that's been swallowed up by the sky. I wish I had a telescope so I could get a better look. It's weird, but in a way the half moon sort of reminds me of Ben — one part open to the world, the other part a dark, shadowy secret.

See, there I go again! This is nuts! There must be *something* I can do to squeeze this guy out of my thoughts. I stare down at the phone that's lying on the floor beside me. If Aunt Su were still here, she'd know how to help. I know this for a fact. Jeepers creepers, my heart hurts just thinking her name. Suddenly, a giant wave of loneliness crashes down over my head. Tears fill my eyes. Here I am, facing imminent death by exhaustion, and not one person on the planet to talk to about my problems.

Crap. I hate feeling sorry for myself.

Blinking away the tears, I reach down, pick up the phone, and push the only number on my speed dial that isn't Aunt Su's.

Ring ... ring ... ring ... ring ... ring...

Click. Pause. And then a very foggy "'Ullo?"

"Dad ... you up?" I can't control a little trill of hope from seeping out into my voice.

"Lily? Z'at you?"

"Yeah."

"Wass wrong?"

"Nothing. Just wanted to talk."

"What time ..." Another pause. I can hear a shuffling of sheets and then a faint bang. "Jeez! Do you realize its three o'clock in the morning?" Dad's voice is quite obviously awake now. I can't help smiling. Maybe he'll actually stay up and talk to me for a bit. Maybe I can even tell him about my sleeping crisis. And Mom's nutty plan to condemn Aunt Su's cabin. Maybe he can help. I take a deep breath.

"Yeah, Dad, I know how late it is."

"What's going on? Are you okay? Is there an emergency?"

I shake my head just as if he can see me through the phone. "No emergency, Dad. Really. I couldn't sleep and I ... I just wanted to talk."

He sighs into his receiver so loudly, I can literally feel the gush of air on my ear.

"Bloody hell ..." I hear him mumble. My smile falls into a frown. I know exactly what's coming next.

"You know I'd love to keep you company, honey. But if I don't get a good night's sleep, my whole day at work will be shot. I've got to be on a conference call at nine and I have back-to-back meetings scheduled for the rest of the day."

My fingers grip the phone so hard, I'm surprised the plastic casing doesn't crack. A second later, I hear him muffle what sounds like an endless yawn. "You understand, don't you, Sweetness?"

I know if I try to speak at that moment, my voice will break apart. So I just nod. As if he can see me through the phone.

"How 'bout you read a book or something to help you get to sleep? And I promise, we'll talk tomorrow."

A *book*? I'm dying from exhaustion and *that's* his best suggestion for me?

Sigh.

"Okay, whatever, Dad." Without even waiting for his goodbye, I click off the phone and let it fall to the floor with a clunk. A second later the guilt police pull up inside my brain. *Crap, why did I just do that? Dad's not like Aunt Su. He needs his rest or he can't function at work. God, this lack of sleep is making me so mean, I can barely stand myself.* My eyes fly up to the night sky. The moon shimmers, like it's trying to cheer me up by being extra beautiful.

"Thanks, buddy," I whisper. Yeah, I must be the only person in history to make friends with the moon. Sounds crazy, right? Well, I don't care. Think what you want. The fact is, the moon is actually an angsty teenager in disguise. S'truth. Just think about it: it's forever hanging back by itself in the sky — as aloof as a floating iceberg. And it's constantly changing and passing in and out of phases. But it always finds a way back to its true self in the end.

"I'd really like to come out there and say hi," I whisper, "but I'm kind of trapped at the moment." I point to the lock on my window for emphasis. "Maybe tomorrow if I can think of a way to bust out of here." The shimmering stops and a thin shadow passes across the glowing, white surface. A frown. My heart swells. Yeah, good friends always have your back.

Good friends.

I glance over at Aunt Su's pomegranate jar, still perched on my desk, and my stomach does a nervous somersault. I feel so guilty about those ashes. For the life of me, I can't seem to figure out what to do with them. For a little while, I was thinking about scattering them in the lake just beyond Aunt Su's circular dock. After all, it was her most favourite place in the world. But then I started imagining her ashes getting gobbled up for breakfast by catfish and frogs and water snakes and that idea shot out the window. And then I thought about taking the jar with me on a moped ride through Big Bend. With the lid open. On a windy day. That way I could just let the ashes fly out on the breeze and fall where they wanted to fall. For about a minute, it seemed like the perfect plan. But then I imagined turning a corner and the jar tipping off the moped and cracking open on the road and all Aunt Su's ashes getting run over and crushed by passing traffic. Not to mention the fact that General MacArthur would probably have me arrested if she knew I was driving a motorized vehicle without a licence. So the moped-scattering idea got turfed pretty quickly too. Now I'm out of ideas and Mom's harping on me big time to get rid of the ashes. Do yourself a favour, my friend: if anyone ever tries to convince you that being responsible for

another person's earthly remains is an easy job, don't listen to
them.

My eyes drop back down to the lock on my window. My
mom's a real piece of work, isn't she? Locking me in my room,
keeping me away from Aunt Su's stuff, threatening to tear down
the cabin. I know General MacArthur's trying to protect me in her
own twisted, obsessive, controlling way, but that doesn't mean I
have to sit back and be a passive prisoner. I make a mental note to
drop by Dad's place on the way home from school tomorrow to
apologize for being such a bitch tonight. While I'm there, I'll take
a look and see if he has a wrench.

Even a sledgehammer will do.

Turning away from the window, I lean over and pick the phone
back up off the floor. Ever have one of those moments where you
feel like you're going to explode out of your skin if you don't hear
another human voice? Yeah, that's me right now.

Flipping onto my side, I click the phone on and dial 4-1-1.
Sometimes, a recorded voice is better than nothing. I wait. Robotic
ringing fills my ear. And then:

"Directory assistance, how may I help you?"

At this time of night I was fully expecting to get a machine,
so imagine my shock to hear a real live person's voice on the
other end. The voice belongs to a woman. Kind of motherly sounding. Not at all tired. Jeepers creepers, why didn't I think of this
before?

"Um, hi ... how are you?" I stammer.

"Fine, thank you." The voice on the other end sounds surprised.
"Person or business?"

"Excuse me?"

The voice slows drastically down, like it's talking to someone
who doesn't speak English.

"Are you looking to find a person or a business?"

I'm not picky, lady, I feel like saying. *Anyone conscious will do fine.* "I'm, well ... before we get to that, can I ask you a question?"

There's a short pause on the line. "Sure, I guess. What kind of question, hon?"

"I just wanted to ask ... well, what time is it where you are?"

I have to know. If she's in China or somewhere on the other side of the world, a live human voice would make a lot more sense. I mean, it's daytime over there, right?

"You want to know what time it is?" she repeats.

"Yes, please."

"It's 3:21 in the morning."

My heart jumps. Same time as here. Maybe this lady lives in Big Bend too! Or somewhere nearby. Maybe she'll stay on the line with me until I fall asleep. This could be the answer to my problems!

"And what's your name?" Introductions are always a good beginning. I mean, you gotta start somewhere, right?

There's another pause. "I'm not really supposed to ..."

My fingers tighten up around the phone. "Please. It's important ..."

She pauses and I can hear the voices of other operators in the background. I'm guessing she must be in a room full of people. Yeah, I'm probably the only person in the world who's ever been jealous of a directory assistance operator. "My name's Frieda, hon," she finally replies. "What's yours?"

Frieda. Good name. A mental image pops into my head. Friendly, plump, greyish curly hair, about Aunt Su's age ...

"My name's Lily," I practically sing. "Lily MacArthur."

More voices in the background fill the bubble of air between us. I'm about to ask her if she can stay on the line with me for a while. I want to know where she lives, and if she has kids and pets, and what books she likes to read, and if she loves her job, and if she ends up sleeping all day long so she can stay up at night ...

But then it all comes crashing down around my head.

"Well, Lily, I wish I could stay and talk to you all night," Frieda's voice is a whisper now. My heart sinks. I know where this is going. "But right now my boss is giving me a look like I'd better get on to my next call if I know what's good for me."

"Oh."

"I'm sorry, hon." And she does sound genuinely sorry. I close my eyes. The mental image of the plump, curly-haired lady melts away.

"S'okay, Frieda." I say.

"Did you still want that number?"

"What? Oh, yeah ... I guess I do."

"Person or business?"

"Um, person. No, scratch that. Business."

"Okay. Want to tell me the name and address, hon?"

"Yeah." I scramble to think of a business I might want to call at this time of night. There's only one that comes to mind. "McCool Fries on Main Street in Big Bend."

"Okay, I'll connect you now."

"Wait, Frieda ..."

I want to say thank you for talking to me. And I want to say sorry for getting her in trouble. But she's gone before I can say anything more. All of a sudden, there's the sound of ringing in my ear. And more ringing.

Crap. What am I doing?

Hang up, Lily. Why are you calling him? You know he's just going to be rude to you. Hang. Up. Now.

A burning knot of anger starts to form in my chest as my mind flips back to our last conversation.

Just. Leave. Me. Alone!

That rage in his voice. And that look of pure panic in his eyes. My index finger hovers over the phone's "off" button, but for some reason I just can't seem to make myself push it. What's wrong with me? He told me to leave him alone. Why can't I do it? I put the receiver back up to my ear. After what feels like an hour, the ringing stops. There's a click. And then a voice. Ben's voice.

"Hello, McCool Fries."

God, he sounds so tired. The knot of anger inside me loosens.

"Hi. It's Lily."

I don't know why, but my throat suddenly feels like tissue paper.

"Hi," he says.

"Yeah, hi."

Ugh. Did I really just say "hi" twice?

Pi-length pause here.

"So, why are you calling?"

Good question. Why exactly am I calling him?

"I-I don't know. I-I ..."

I can't finish that sentence — my mind is suddenly, totally, completely blank. I can feel my cheeks start to spark and for a moment I'm seriously thinking about hanging up and forgetting I ever knew a boy named Ben Matthews. And then he says this:

"S'okay. I'm glad you called. I was actually thinking about you."

It's like hot chocolate with marshmallows sliding into my ears, each word warming every single millimetre of me up from the inside out.

"You were?"

"Unh-huh."

It takes a few seconds to swallow the sticky wad of nerves rising in my esophagus.

"So ... I didn't wake you up?"

"Don't worry about it."

"Okay ..."

There's a long, surprisingly easy silence. I hear Death Cab for Cutie playing in the background and then the voice of a radio DJ announcing the next song. I bend my head toward the window and stare out at my moon. It's tinted yellow tonight — the colour of parched grass.

"It's so late. I wasn't sleeping ..."

The mention of sleep brings out a long, yodel-sounding yawn from the phone. "Yeah, about that. I did a bit of research on your problem."

My mouth falls open. "Y-you did?"

"I did." Another yodel yawn. "And I found out some pretty freaky stuff. Do you know that people who are seriously sleep deprived usually suffer from anxiety, blurred vision, slurred speech, and concentration lapses?"

Don't forget the heart palpitations, I think to myself.

"Not to mention hallucinations and paranoia," he continues.

Hallucinations? My thoughts reel backward to the moment the drive-thru speaker morphed into a snarling panther. Suddenly it feels like there's a knife pushing into my chest. "In other words, they go crazy. Is that what you're saying?"

"Uh, yeah, I guess you could look at it that way."

Great! As if I'm not strange enough already. Now I have to add "imminent insanity" to my growing list of problems. Just call me the "odd girl out of time."

"So, how many days did you say it's been now?" Ben asks.

"Twenty-five."

I think I hear him whistle through the phone. "And have you been having any of those symptoms?"

I just can't bring myself to tell him the awful truth about the panther hallucination. Or the heart flutters either, for that matter.

"I guess I have been pretty grumpy. More than usual, I mean."

For a few seconds, all I can hear is the sound of my own breath in the receiver.

"Yeah, I've been sort of grumpy too. I'm sorry for yelling at you the other day at school. I've been ... I just haven't felt like myself lately. I guess this graveyard shift thing is getting to me."

"Thanks."

His apology makes me feel a bit better. But I can still hear those secrets in his voice. I know there's so much he's not telling me.

"Hey, want to come by the drive-thru?" he says. "We could take another walk to the Docks. I can make a fresh batch of fries."

Yes, I want to come so badly. I look at the lock on my window and my eyes fill with tears. I shake my head. I'm impossibly imprisoned. And even if I wasn't, Ben needs his sleep.

"No, not tonight."

I wait for him to say goodbye and hang up. Go back to his nap and leave me alone with the night. Instead, he says, "I want to help you, Lily. Help, you know, figure out this sleep thing."

His voice is tender and soft — like a goose-down pillow against my ear. My throat feels tight. It sounds just like something Aunt Su would have said.

I flop back onto the mattress. My arm comes up to cover my eyes like a blindfold. *I'm running out of time, Ben. At this point, I seriously doubt anyone's going to be able to help me find my sleep.*

I don't say that.

But I do say this: "Why do you want to help me? I mean, half the time I'm not even sure you even like me."

"I do like you." His voice is just a hum now.

"Why?"

Short pause.

"I think because you're different. I mean, every single thing about you is like nothing I've ever known. Does that make sense?"

Blood floods my brain. I shake my head, trying to chase off a sudden rush of wooziness. "No. No sense at all."

"It's just, you make me feel things ... see things ... I don't know how to explain it."

Someone's poured a bucketful of sand down my throat. "Try," I somehow manage to squeak.

Another hour seems to pass while I wait for his answer.

"Everything's different when I'm with you," he finally says. "I-I like it."

Different. Difference. *You'll make a difference in someone's life, Lily-girl.* That's what Aunt Su wrote. In her suicide note.

Aunt Su.

The cabin.

I sit back up.

"I guess there is one thing you could help me with Ben, but it's not about sleep."

"Okay, what?"

"This is going to sound strange, but you wouldn't happen to know anything about repairing old buildings, would you?"

A big blob of silence oozes into my ear. So big that, for a moment, I actually think Ben's hung up.

"Hello?" I whisper into the phone.

"Yeah. I'm still here," he whispers back.

"So?"

"So, what do you want to know?"

A Short and Very Excited Note from Me

You're not going to believe this! So, it looks like I finally found out Ben's secret. Well, one of them at least. Turns out his dad owns a construction business. And not just any old construction business; it's the biggest bloody one in the whole entire province. Ben is supposed to take it over one day and he has a bunch of builder friends who might be able to help me with the repair. He's going to stop by the cabin this Sunday for a quick look and tell me what I need to do to get it up to safety standards.

I feel like laughing. Ha! Take that, General MacArthur!

And singing. No white flags above my door, Mom!

And dancing. With Aunt Su's pomegranate jar. Around and around and around.

And so I will.

Toodle-oo ...

SIXTEEN

September 20th

Emma. Again.

I see her red hair approaching out of the corner of my eye. Bounce, bounce ... wave, smile. For the first time all month, I don't cringe at the sight of her glee. In fact, after just a dewdrop of hesitation, I actually shift my Arial Narrow butt a millimetre to the left to make room for her Curlz. A puff of perfumed wind rises up as she drops onto the cafeteria bench beside me.

"Hey, Lil!"

I push a bit of nice into my voice. "Hey, Em."

And I even manage to smile back at her. *Hey, look at me!*

She plops her lunch bag onto the table. It sits there for a moment, all bulging and round, like a brown paper stomach pouch. Then, one by one, she begins extracting the contents.

Egg salad sandwich. "So, have you heard the latest buzz?"

I shake my head. "Hardly."

Granny Smith apple. "Apparently, Todd's pretty torn up about you."

I practically choke on a mouthful of chocolate milk. "Excuse me ... what did you just say?"

Ziplock of baby carrots. "Yeah, seems like he's gone all emo over your ass."

"Could you just rewind, please? Are you talking about Todd *Nelson*?"

Chocolate pudding and white plastic spoon. "Wake up, Lily. Of course I'm talking about Todd Nelson. Did you make out with any other Todds at this school?"

I can tell by the edge in Emma's voice that she's getting impatient with me. *Wow, quel grand switch!* She pulls out the final item from the bag (orange soda) then begins flattening the paper out for recycling. Her next words come out big and rounded — like a row of giant gumballs: "Funny how you never told me what happened between you guys after I left you by the pool."

Emma leans a bit closer to hear my answer. Her brown eyes are practically begging for details. *Oh my God, what is she thinking?* "Nothing happened!" I say, a little louder maybe than necessary. "Absolutely nothing!"

"Really?" She straightens back up. "Sorry, but based on the evidence, I have a hard time believing that," she replies, peeling open the foil top of her pudding and licking it clean.

"What evidence?"

Emma smiles. "Oh, I don't know. How 'bout the fact that he's been wandering around looking like a funeral director since the weekend?"

"What? Not because of me!"

"Yeah, I'm pretty sure. I heard some guys teasing him about his big crush in gym today and they mentioned your name. It sounded like they couldn't believe it either. No offence or anything."

You could have knocked me over with a sneeze. To my knowledge, no guy (or girl, for that matter) has ever had a fraction of an interest in me before. My thoughts skip back to that night by the pool. Todd's beery, panting breath. His fumbly fingers on my bra. His slobbery mouth. I reach up to wipe the memory of his spit off my lips. "It was next to redundant. Just a kiss. Honestly."

"And then?"

"And then nothing. We kissed. He wanted more, but I didn't." My stomach is heaving just talking about it. "And then I left before anything could, you know, go too far. I went straight home. End of story."

Emma scoops a spoonful of chocolate into her mouth. "Okay. That was sincere. Now I believe you." Her red eyebrows arch halfway up her forehead. "But Todd's pretty cute, you know."

"I know."

Another scoop. "And nice. And smart."

"Yeah, I know."

She swirls her spoon around and around in the pudding. And then she starts nodding like it all makes so much sense. Infuriating. "*What?*"

"Nothing. I just *get* it now."

"Get *what?*" Crap, why does it feel like we're not even speaking the same language here?

Emma sighs, like a parent dealing with a bratty kid. "What's going on with Todd. I get the whole thing. It's pretty obvious, actually."

Holy cow! I want to grab those ringlets and wrap them around her polka-dotted neck! "Could you just explain it to me, then?"

"It's just basic human nature, really. You're the unattainable and Todd's all worked up about it. People always want what they think they can't have. Simple."

I'm the unattainable. I can feel my irritation start to fade. *Okay, yeah, I like that.*

"I learned all about it on the Discovery Channel last summer," she continues. "Every mammal on the planet is genetically pro-grammed for the chase. Which, I'm guessing, is the exact reason why you left Todd high and dry at the party? Am I right?"

Her eyebrows shoot up suggestively. *Oh God, she's talking*

about Ben. I can feel the straight line of my mouth slowly widening into a perfect circle of shock. How did she figure it out? Am I that transparent? My eyes do a quick sweep of the cafeteria, searching for him. He's not there.

Relief.

I lean closer to Emma and lower my voice to whisper. "When we're not in school — when we're alone — he's different. I swear, he's actually nice." My thoughts skip back to that night on the beach when he brought me an ice cream bar. And gave me his jacket to keep warm. And tried to stop me from going into Todd's wild party. And his offer to help me find my sleep again. And fix up the cabin. "It's not just that. He's caring too."

Emma nods and offers me a baby carrot. "And, just to be clear, I'm assuming you've noticed how genetically blessed he is?"

Man, why is it suddenly so warm in here? "Yeah, of course. I'm not blind, you know." I take the carrot from Emma and crunch down loudly. It tastes like cold cardboard, but I keep chewing. "But there's more to it than just that. I ... I think he's in trouble. He comes off as this big, unsolvable mystery. And it's like there's something he needs and he's angry he doesn't have it and he's aching to get it. But he doesn't even know what it is." Forcing down the icky mouthful of carrot, I drop my face into my hands so nobody else can see the burning that's growing in my cheeks. "God, did that make any kind of sense?"

"Yup."

I look up from my hands. I can't explain how, but the freckles on Emma's face are suddenly all adding up to an answer — like the final picture in a connect-the-dots puzzle.

"You think I should go talk to him and tell him how I feel, right?"

She nods and hands me another carrot. "I don't know what you're waiting for. You know where to find him."

"I'm supposed to see him on Sunday."

"Why wait? I mean, why don't you go to McCool's tonight?"

"Tonight?" My pulse races just thinking about it. She's right — I need to talk to him. Alone. And not on the phone this time. But how am I going to get past General MacArthur and her army of security devices? I shake my head. "Can't do it. My mother banned me from going out at night anymore. She even put locks on my room and everything."

I wait for her to finish crushing another baby carrot with her teeth. "Well, I know an easy enough way around that," she finally says.

My jaw drops open. *An easy way around Operation Teen Lockdown?* "What?"

With a devilish grin, Emma flings an arm around my shoulder and pulls my angles into her curves. "Lily MacArthur, you're about to go on your first sleepover."

SEVENTEEN

The General turned out to be easy as pie to convince. For Pete's sake, she even helped me pack my overnight bag (all except for one highly confidential item). A sleepover at an honest-to-goodness friend's house? Forget about the fact that she'd grounded me; she's been praying for this day since I was born and there was no way in hell she was going to let me miss it. Believe you me. I mean, here I was on the verge of turning sixteen, finally doing something she considered "normal." I could practically hear her victory thoughts as she dropped me off at Emma's house. *Hallelujah! Crack open the champagne!* Her lifelong fantasy of having a halfway-human daughter was finally coming true! I'm just shocked she didn't bring her video camera to record the moment for all eternity.

Sheesh.

What did I tell you about parents and normalcy? I wouldn't be surprised if Mom goes and calls up all her friends to brag about my sleepover as soon as she gets home.

Anyway, it's just after nine o'clock when I get to the Swartzes' house. As soon as Mom is gone and my sneakers are off, Emma takes my hand and drags me upstairs to her bedroom. Her hair is divided into two red squirrely pigtails and she's wearing a pair of pink flannel unicorn pyjamas. Very fuzzy and girly and fun. Suddenly, I'm so nervous I think I might vomit. Green chunks all over her pink bunny slippers. The mental image of it brings a smile to my face. Unfortunately, Emma takes that as a sign of encouragement and starts dragging me faster.

"Wait a minute," I yelp. "You're not going to make me watch *High School Musical*, are you?"

She shakes her head so hard, her curly pigtails slap against her face. "Unh-unh. I have something else in mind."

She pushes open the door to her bedroom with an exaggerated *Ta-da!* I hold my breath and peek inside, certain on some instinctive level that I'm going to abhor what's in there. Turns out I'm right. Her room is like something out of a corny teen movie. The four-poster canopy bed is the first thing I see. It stands out like a massive monument to Pepto-Bismol in its pink, frothy glory. A collection of pop music posters papers the walls from floor to ceiling. There's a small bookcase under the window crammed with books. The ones I can see from the doorway have shiny, bright covers and smiling teenagers.

I guess it could have been worse. I mean, at least she's gotten rid of the Barbies.

"We have a lot to do and not much time to do it in, so I think we should get started right away," Emma says, pointing to a chipped orange stool beside the doorway.

"Hunh? Get started with what?"

Don't laugh! My introversion, you understand, has left me pathetically unaware of the traditional slumber party transformative ritual. A moment later, it all becomes clear when I notice what's sitting directly in front of the chipped orange stool: a small table set with makeup cases, small, candy-coloured nail-polish bottles, an array of beaded jewellery, a bottle of Justin Bieber perfume, and a purple brush with a matching comb. Tweezers, curlers, and various other unidentifiable instruments of torture have been ominously laid out beside an electrical outlet. The realization of what Emma's plotting falls over me like a giant spider web. She takes a step toward me, a can of hairspray clutched in her hand.

Final Net.

How apropos.

I take a step back. "Maybe this sleepover thing isn't such a good idea."

But she grabs my arm before I can bolt. "Come on, Lily! Makeovers are what sleepovers are all about!"

"No!" I try to pull my arm away, but she's stronger than she looks. "Let me go!"

"Aren't you even the least bit curious to see how good you could look?"

"No!"

"Would you stop acting so stubborn?"

"*No!*"

She stomps her bunny-slippered foot on the floor and gestures at me with the can of Final Net. "Well, you're not going to go spill your heart out to Ben Matthews looking like *that*, are you?"

Ben. Just the sound of his name makes my heart leap up into my throat. I look down at myself. Track pants and the holey tie-dyed Grateful Dead T-shirt I've been wearing since yesterday. I lean my head down and take a sniff. My entire body sags with defeat.

"Okay, no. I guess not." Giving up, I let my muscles relax into spaghetti noodles as Emma pushes me down onto the stool. Her freckles are practically dancing with happiness.

"You're going to love it, I promise!"

"I highly doubt that, but *fine*. Just a little bit."

And so I do it. I close my eyes and let Emma Swartz have her way with me. For the next hour, she powders and polishes and plucks and plastic attacks me. I let her do it without any more complaining — I guess it feels like, in a way, I'm making up for ruining her Barbies all those years ago.

Karma's *une salope*.

When she's done, I open my eyes, look into the mirror, and scream.

Emma's freckles sag with disappointment. "You don't like it?"

"No! I look hideous!" I lean closer to examine the monster in the mirror. There isn't even a trace of my former self behind all the colour and gloss and pouf she's poured over me.

"But you look like a movie star," Emma whines.

"I don't want to look like a movie star. I want to look like me!"

"Don't be that way, Lily."

"Get it off, now!"

I make her take it all off and do it again, with a decimal point's worth of stuff this time. She grumbles and groans to let me know she doesn't approve. But she does it anyway.

Just as she's finishing up, Mrs. Swartz pops her head in the doorway. She has short brown hair, bright blue eyes, and a perfectly spherical body. She's actually quite the geometric marvel — for the life of me, I can't tell where her bosom ends and her stomach begins. She's so full of curve, she manages to make Emma look angular. Not an easy feat, believe you me.

"Goodnight, girls, I'm heading to bed," she says with a wide, half-circle smile. "Your makeup looks lovely, Lily. Very natural." I see her glance down at her watch. "But you're not planning on going out at this hour, are you?"

I freeze on my stool. Does she know I'm planning on going out to meet Ben? Will she lock us in Emma's room for the night? Or even worse, call my house and tell the General? *Yikes.* But lucky for me, Cool Emma isn't fazed in the slightest. She just twirls the comb around her fingers like a mini-baton and laughs.

"No, of course not. We're just playing around with the makeup."

Très nonchalant.

Mrs. Swartz stifles a yawn. "Okay, well, have fun. Don't stay up too late."

The second the door closes, I breathe a sigh of relief. Emma points the comb at my body and wrinkles her nose like a pug dog.

"Okay ... now, for your wardrobe."

Before I can officially protest, she strides over to her closet and comes out holding up an armful of clothes. "I borrowed a few things from my sister's room before you got here. She's small and scrawny like you, so I'm guessing these will be close to your size."

Next thing I know, she's dressing me up in one of her little sister's pairs of skinny jeans and a baby blue T-shirt with the words "Clearly Misunderstood" printed across the front.

Oxymoronic. Okay, I can handle that. I pull on the clothes and plunk myself back down on the stool.

"Fine, I'm dressed. What now?"

"Now we wait for my dad to go to sleep. Then we sneak you out."

Her work done for the night, Emma flops onto her bed and cuddles up with a squishy-looking pink heart pillow.

"So what are you going to do about Todd? It's not cool to leave him hanging like a lovesick puppy, you know."

My stomach feels like it's just dropped down an elevator shaft. "I'll think of something. But not now — tomorrow, after I talk to Ben."

Emma tilts her head and studies my face. "You look nervous. Have you figured out what you're going to say?"

Shrug. "I don't know. Maybe I'll just wing it." After a small pause, I add, "Or maybe I'll borrow a line or two from *this*." With a grin, I reach for my overnight bag and pull out my one highly confidential item: my dog-eared copy of *Summer of Love*. Emma's eyes widen the second she spots the half-naked bodies of Jason and Amy cavorting on the cover.

"Oh my God! Where did you get that?"

"It's one of Aunt Su's romance novels. I found it in her cabin. I'm not finished it yet, but so far there's lots of juicy stuff." I open it up and start flipping to the end of the first chapter. "I marked all of the best scenes to show you. But this one's my favourite so far." I open my mouth to start reading about what Jason and Amy do at the end of their first date. But before I know what's happening, Emma is sprinting across the room and grabbing the book out of my hands.

"Holy crap! I can't believe you got a copy of this! Dad won't let me read these books 'til I'm sixteen!" She skips through the pages on high speed, as if the book is about to dissolve any second.

"Hey, be careful," I warn, reaching to take it back. "That's practically an antique, you know."

But that's when Emma pauses and pulls the book closer to her face. Her thin red eyebrows come together like a pinch.

"Look, I think your aunt put one of her little drawings in this one too."

"What?"

She holds up the book for me to see, spread open to show the inside back cover. I lean closer and peer at the page. There's a cartoon drawn in purple ink of two shadowy figures standing and holding hands on top of a mountain peak. The sky above them is filled with tiny flowers.

Lilies.

Suddenly, it feels like there's a cool breeze blowing over my insides. "Let me see that," I say, grabbing the book back from Emma. My eyes scrape over the page as my heart cartwheels against my ribcage.

It's definitely a note from Aunt Su — dated almost exactly a month ago. The day of her suicide.

"It's a note for me," I whisper. And then I start to read in my head.

Lily-girl,

I know if you've found this note, it means you're reading my books. And if you're reading my books, it means you're not mad at me anymore for what I've done. And if you're not mad at me anymore, then maybe you'll be open to hearing one last piece of advice — believe me when I say it's the most important piece of advice I'll ever offer you. Now that I've reached the end of this life, I can honestly say that my only regret is how much I disconnected myself from the world. To be a writer, I chose a life of solitude when I was young and pushed almost everyone (with the wonderful exception of you and one or two dear friends) away from me so I could have the freedom to follow my dreams. Looking back, I know I would have had a fuller life if I'd filled it more with people instead of silence and space. Lily-girl, I know your way is to push others away, just like mine was. And of course, you should follow your writing dreams. But at the same time, be sure to find a place for family, friends, and love. When you get to the end of the road, it's the only thing that matters.

Your ever adoring Aunt.

Suddenly, I feel Emma's hand land on my shoulder. "So, what does it say?" Her voice is soft with concern. I cough to clear away the nest of prickles that has sprouted inside my throat.

"It's something Aunt Su wrote before she died. She's just ... she's just telling me how much she loves me." I angle my body away so she won't see the tears. Her hand squeezes my shoulder gently.

"Are you okay, Lily?"

"Yeah, I'm fine … thanks." I take a second to wipe at my eyes and shove the book back into my bag. "But it's late — I should probably get going soon if I want to see Ben …"

Emma releases my shoulder just long enough to check her watch. "It's almost midnight. I'm sure my dad will be going to bed any time now. He likes to stay up late reading. Shouldn't be too much longer. You're not getting tired, are you?"

I laugh at that. *Hard.* Yeah, I laugh so hard, I almost pee my borrowed pair of little sister pants. And Emma laughs along with me, even though she has no idea why. It's a cheek-smarting, mouth-stretching, hold-your-stomach-and-cross-your-legs-so-you-don't-have-an-accident kind of laugh. And it's so much better than anything I've felt in a long, *long* time.

Finally, after a few minutes, Emma catches her breath enough to ask: "So w-what's so funny, anyway?"

"I … I don't sleep. Like, at all. I kind of lost it after my Aunt Su died. I don't know where it went. And I'm kind of beginning to think I'll never find it again."

Silence with a side order of confused frownage. "What, you don't sleep at *all*?"

"Nope."

"Not even a catnap?"

Vigorous shake.

Emma whistles as she wipes a stray strand of hair out of her face. "God, Lily, I didn't think that was humanly possible."

"It is … but just for eighteen days."

"What happens after eighteen days?"

"You die."

"And how many days has it been for you?"

"Twenty-six."

"Seriously?"

Nod.

"Why aren't you dead?"

My voice shrinks down to a tiny whisper. "I don't know. I'm pretty sure I'm a genetic anomaly."

Emma smiles and air-pokes me from across the room. "Yeah. I knew there was a reason I liked you."

And that's it. No doubts, no arguments, no thinly veiled looks of scepticism. I wait for her to tell me I'm crazy, that it's impossible, that I must be lying. But she doesn't. Instead, she just squishes her heart pillow in half to make a shelf for her chin and silently believes me. Just like the main character's best buddy inside all those cheesy teen books lined up on Emma's shelf.

Who knew stuff like that actually happens in real life?

For the second time tonight, I feel the tears coming on and don't know how to stop them. Oh God, I'm so terrified I can barely think straight. Terrified of dying, of losing the cabin, of having my first real friend, of telling Ben how I feel, and of him not feeling the same way about me. I turn towards the wall and swipe my hands over my eyes. My breath stutters painfully in my throat.

"Lily, are you okay?"

I nod, mopping the last of the tears with the hem of my borrowed T-shirt. Before I can say anything, there's another knock at the door. We both turn to see Mr. Swartz poking his head into the room. "You girls still up?"

Picture an older, male version of Emma and you'll get a good idea of what Mr. Swartz looks like. The similarity is kind of eerie, actually. Except his red hair has streaks of silver winding through the curls. And his freckles have all joined together to make a ruddy looking tan. Plus he's wearing a pair of those funny old-person reading glasses that look like half-moons. I recognize him vaguely from the few times I'd gone browsing inside Beachside

Books. And I think I probably saw him at Aunt Su's funeral reception too — but pretty much everyone in Big Bend had charged through our house that day, so that's kind of a given.

"Well, for goodness' sake! Lily MacArthur? Is that you?" Mr. Swartz walks into the room and reaches for my hand. "It's so nice to see you!"

Did I mention the fact that his eyebrows are totally fused together in the middle of his forehead? It looks like there's a long, bushy, red caterpillar sleeping on top of his nose. Just as I'm opening my mouth to speak, the caterpillar opens its beady little eyes and smiles at me.

"Thanks," I reply, pulling my hand back. "It's ... um, nice to see you too, Mr. Swartz."

Mr. Swartz and his caterpillar are both staring at me so intensely. Makes me feel like a bug under a microscope. "You look all grown up with that makeup! Is that my daughter's doing?"

I hear Emma groan beside me. "Dad, please!"

"Sorry Em." Chuckle, chuckle. "It's just that I always think of Lily as Su's little niece."

Now the caterpillar is chuckling too. A line of shivers runs up my spine. *Is this another hallucination? Man, I really hope so.* I take a small step back. Mr. Swartz takes a small one forward.

"I was a good friend of your aunt's, you know?"

I swallow hard. "Yeah, she went to your bookstore a lot, right?"

The caterpillar rises up and starts hopping up and down his forehead. "That, she did," Mr. Swartz replies. "We've been friends for years and years."

"Really?" *Why can't I remember her mentioning him?*

"Really. And she talked about you constantly. I have, in fact, been hearing all about you since the day you were born."

Right then, my guts feel like they'd been dropped onto the floor. And then stomped on. And then set on fire. *Where have I heard*

*those exact same words recently? And why do they make me feel
so icky inside?* But before I have the chance to figure it out, Emma
has her hands on his shoulders and is pushing Mr. Swartz back
toward the doorway. "Time for you to go now, Dad. This is a girls
only night, remember?"

He holds up a hand to stop her. "Actually, Em, I think I'd like
to have a moment alone with Lily."

Alone?

"Dad …" There's a hint of a warning crouched behind Emma's
words. Jeepers creepers, why is this night suddenly making no
sense? It feels like I'm trapped in some kind of weird, dystopian
nightmare. But of course, that would be impossible because only
people who sleep are allowed to have nightmares. *Sucks to be me.*

"Don't worry, Em, it won't be long," he says. "I just want to
have a little chat about Su." In a split second, everything goes and
flips upside down. Now Mr. Swartz is the one pushing Emma out
the door. I leap forward before she can leave, frantically trying
to signal her with my eyes. Morse code eyelid blinks — everyone
knows how to decipher those, right?

No, don't go, Emma, I blink desperately.

She pauses.

Yes! It worked!

"Is the mascara bothering you, Lily?"

*Merde! No. No. No. Don't leave me alone with your dad and
his freaky caterpillar!* I blink again.

"Hmmm, I'll see if we have a fresh box of tissues. Be back in
a minute."

And then she's gone. The door closes behind her with an ominous snap. Mr. Swartz reaches for my hand again.

"How you doing, honey?"

I back away. Across the room to Emma's big, pink bed. *Why
is he asking me that? And why is he calling me honey?* "Yeah,

thanks ... I'm good." Now the warning has settled in behind *my* words. Hopefully he hears it. And maybe he does because he doesn't try to come after me or take my hand again. Instead, he just talks.

Relief.

"I know it must have been quite shocking to hear the news about your aunt."

I grip onto one of the bed's posts. "Yeah, sure."

Mr. Swartz's voice suddenly shrinks down to a whisper. "Believe me, I would rather have told you in person instead of in a letter. But I think it was important for Su to let you know the truth her own words."

What letter? "What letter?"

"The one from your aunt. I mailed it to your father's house after the funeral." The bushy red caterpillar, which had been lying still for the past minute, suddenly starts hunching down over Mr. Swartz's eyes. "You *did* get my letter, didn't you?"

The letter. Oh my God! That's why this guy's giving me such ick! He's the strange old person with the stamp who isn't my friend! The writer of the first white letter! Aunt Su's suicide note suddenly comes rushing back to me like a fierce gust of wind. My knees wobble and I sink down onto the end of Emma's frothy bed. I get that funny, bitter taste at the back of my mouth. You know the taste I'm talking about? The one that makes you think your dinner is moments away from making a reappearance on the floor? I white-knuckle the bedpost and focus hard on the Pepto-Bismol pink. *Please, let it be okay.*

Deep breath in. Deep breath out.

A bit better.

Mr. Swartz's caterpillar is peering at me over the rim of his half-moon glasses. "Lily, honey? Are you all right?"

No, not even close. "Yes, Mr. Swartz, I did get the letter."

He takes a fraction of a step forward. This time, I don't mind so much. This guy is Aunt Su's friend, after all. She trusted him with her biggest secret. It's okay for me to trust him too.

"I'm just so glad you and Emma have become friends," he says. "I knew it would be a good idea for you two to reconnect."

"Um, you did?"

The caterpillar climbs up his forehead — like it's looking for a safe place to build its cocoon. "Don't take it the wrong way. It's just that, you know, after getting the news about your aunt, I figured you could use a friend."

My stomach suddenly feels like I've swallowed a hornet's nest.

"Y-you asked Emma to be my friend?"

The answer is right there on his reddening face. I mean, you could power a city from the heat radiating off his cheeks. My hands curl into fists at my sides. I'm centimetres away from hitting this guy. No, make that millimetres. Aunt Su's friend or not, what he did was so vastly wrong on so many levels. Maybe Mr. Swartz senses my prickly mood, because he ends our private tête-à-tête right there.

"Well, I'll let you go. I can see this is bringing back some powerful memories for you. But please keep in touch. You're welcome to come by the store whenever you're in the neighbourhood. I'll tell you some old stories about your aunt."

Rigid, tight-lipped, signature General MacArthur nod. The hornets in my stomach buzz angrily. The caterpillar on Mr. Swartz's forehead seems to have gone back to sleep. He reaches for the door knob. "Okay, guess I'll go get Emma now."

Did I mention that I'm prone to great acts of stupidity when I'm angry?

The second his back is turned, I'm off the bed and out the window. Justlikethat. The landing pad beneath Emma's bedroom isn't nearly as soft as the one beneath mine. The ground rises up to hit me with a smash. Twin lightning bolts shoot up my legs from the impact. I take a few seconds to shake off the pain, just like Mom taught me to do all those years ago.

And then I start to run.

EIGHTEEN

The sky is black with clouds. No moon to light the way as I take off down the road. Not even a hint of a trace of a sliver. Still, it helps to know it's up there somewhere. Yeah, there are times in life when faith is the only thing you've got. I know this for a fact.

Emma is only pretending to be your friend, chants a nasty little voice in my right ear. *Do you really think she cares about a not-even-halfway-normal, forever-a-disappointment, oxymoronically named, and permanently introverted nocturnal mutant like you? Her father told her to do it.*

Does that make Emma the pathetic one? Or me? I'm too upset to know for sure.

Who cares why she did it? whispers the voice in my other ear. *Fact is, she was your friend ... is your friend. Emma made an effort, when nobody else would. Doesn't she get points for that?*

"Justshutupshutupshutup!" I yell at the voices, shaking my head to knock them loose from my ears. I pick up the pace in case they're planning on following me. Crunch ... crunch ... crunch go my shoes on the gravel as I stumble through the darkness. Past Derry's, past Beachy Keen, past the Spotted Dick, all the way to the one place in the world I need to be. Ignoring the hissing speaker, I go straight to the window of the crappy little cubicle.

I don't care if I wake him up. I don't care how grumpy he'll be. I just have to see him.

But when I look through the window, it isn't him at all. *Merde. It's another one of those hallucinations. It has to be. This is exactly the kind of thing that happens when you don't sleep for twenty-six days.* I close my eyes and shake my head, trying to knock my brain back to reality. But when I open my eyes again a few seconds later, it still isn't Ben. I can feel my chest twisting with dread. This is no hallucination.

"Where is he?" I demand.

Jake Hudson, a senior from my high school, lowers his BlackBerry and frowns.

"Lily MacArthur? Where's your car? This is a drive-thru, you know?"

I'm running out of patience. Fast. "What are you doing here?" I holler at him. "Where's Ben?"

He shrugs. "How should I know? He just pulled me aside today and offered me the shift. Said it was the easiest job in the world. This is my first night."

"When will he be back?" My words are like poisonous darts. But sadly, this guy isn't sharp enough to notice. It's a well-known fact that Jake Hudson has failed grade eleven twice. Not exactly the brightest star in the galaxy.

He shakes his thick head and shrugs again. "Ben won't be back. He quit."

Ben quit? Why? Where did he go? He wouldn't have moved back to Toronto without telling me. *Would he?* In a flash, my angry voice dissolves into an anxious whine.

"But ... do you know where he went? I mean, did he take another job?"

"Sorry, I don't know anything about it," says Jake. "Can I get you some fries? There's a fresh batch ..."

I turn away before he can finish his sentence. Across the parking lot over to the Docks, back through the strip, I march — eyes sweeping the village for Ben. But everything is shut down like a blackout. There's no sign of him anywhere. If I knew where he lived, I'd go to his house. But I don't know where he lives. In fact, I know almost nothing about him. I take to the main road, all the while trying to tell myself it doesn't matter, that I don't care if he's gone. Why should I care, anyway? I barely know the guy! And what I do know isn't all that great. I'll be better off without having to avoid his scowling face at school. Truly. And now I'm free to go get some fries at three o'clock in the morning without worrying about running into His Grumpiness.

For some weird reason, that last thought makes me unbearably sad. Tears burn my eyes. I break into a jog that quickly turns into a run that quickly grows into a frantic gallop. I race down the road as if an invisible monster is on my tail. And the tears keep coming, no matter how fast I try to outrun them. Blinded by the darkness, I don't even know where I'm running until I find myself back on Aunt Su's front lawn. Even through the pitch black sky, I know where I am by the familiar sweet smell of mint in the air. Also by the fact that I trip over the obnoxious, hairy gnome. It's so dark, I can barely make out the shape of the house, but I know it's there. This little cabin has pulled me towards it like a giant magnet. I stumble around to the back, almost totally blinded by the night. The sound of the waves lapping up against the circular dock is almost as familiar as my aunt's voice. I close my eyes and struggle to find my breath.

In ... out ... in ... out ...

Better.

Then ...

A sudden snap of a twig to my right. A cold touch of something brushing against my arm. A shiver crawling up my spine. And

then the sinister hint of an invisible monster's breath blowing on
my skin, stealing my own breath right from my mouth.

Oh my God!

With a yank, I pull my arm away and start running again.
Heart pounding, breath panting, lungs exploding. The cool night
air is suddenly thick, hot, burning against my skin. There's barely
enough of it to pull into my lungs. My feet punch the ground as
I fly up the road. The chomping footsteps of the stranger behind
me fill my heart with ice cold terror. *Don't look. Don't look! He'll
catch you if you turn around to look!*

I can't help it. I turn around to look. Dark shadows everywhere. It's too black to see much of anything, which just makes it
worse because I can hear him following right on my heels. How
can this lunatic see me through the darkness? Is he some serial
psychopath who's invested in night goggles or something? This
latest thought jacks my panic up to a whole new level.

Oh my God! He can see in the dark! He's going to catch me! I
want to scream. Believe you me, I know it's my only defence. I try
so hard to scream.

Help! Somebody help! There's a lunatic chasing me!

The words are so clear in my head, but for the life of me I can't
push them out. My voice is frozen in my throat. Caught up inside
my panicked breath. If I want to live, I'll have to keep running
until I find a house. But my poor muscles are screeching at me to
give up. *There are no neighbours for kilometres, Lily!* And at the
same time, there's a logical little voice somewhere at the back of
my brain calmly informing me I'll never make it. *Let it go. Drop
out of the race. You're dying a slow death-by-exhaustion anyway
— why not let this serial psychopath put you out of your misery?*

What choice do I have? Truly, it's almost a relief to do it. My
muscles serenade me with a chorus of love songs as I let my feet
slow up their pace. Little sparks of light swirl in front of my eyes.

Another second and his cold hands will be around my throat, squeezing the breath right out of my body. I let the serenade take over my thoughts and brace myself for a final, violent end. I've managed to survive for twenty-six days with no sleep and this crazed lunatic with hi-tech night-vision goggles is about to finish me off on a dark, lonely road.

Quel injustice!

My whole body hurts at the thought of never seeing Ben again.

Then, suddenly, out of the darkness comes a beam of light. Shining through my eyes to the back of my skull — blinding me more absolutely than any darkness. I stumble over my feet and feel myself crashing down onto the gravel road. Little stones cut through the knees of my jeans and slice into the skin of my palms. Like miniature teeth.

And then a voice.

"Lily? Is that you?"

NINETEEN

Ben jumps off his bike and kneels down beside me on the gravel. *Crunch* go his shoes on the road. *Boom* goes the pulse in my ears. The smell of watermelon suddenly fills my nose. I close my eyes. My head is spinning so fast, I feel like it might just roll off my body.

"What happened, Lily?"

He's so close, I can feel his words on my face. There isn't even a trace of boredom in his voice. This is new.

"S-someone was chasing me," I manage to say.

I feel him take my hands into his. His fingertips brush over the tiny rocks embedded into my palms.

"You're hurt."

The spinning is beginning to slow a bit. I try to sit up. "We better go. Whoever was chasing me is probably still out here."

His hand presses gently down on my shoulder. "Not yet. Just relax for a minute and catch your breath. There's nobody else out here. Trust me, I was watching from my bike. I saw you running alone down the road."

My lids fly open. "No, that's not true. There was a lunatic on my heels. I heard the footsteps."

"What you heard was probably an echo, Lily. The lake's right beside us."

I peer through the darkness. The lake. Suddenly, the booming in my ears fades and I can hear the waves smacking against the rocks. Is there a chance he's right? What if I was running away from my own footsteps? But I heard him running ... saw his shadow ... felt his breath on me. Was it another hallucination? *Merde!* The paranoia is finally taking over!

This must be the end.

Oh my God!

"You're still bleeding," Ben says, holding my hands up to the light shining off his bike. "We need to wash these cuts out."

I feel an arm circle around my waist. A second later I'm on my feet.

Whoa!

The ground shifts slightly. The circle around me tightens.

"Are you okay? Do you think you can walk?"

Deep breath.

"Yeah, of course." I take a small step to prove it. "See?"

But his arm stays glued in place. "Listen, I think the best idea is to take you to the lake and get you cleaned up."

I don't argue. Ben starts herding me toward the sound of the water, holding me up the whole time. Squinting through the darkness, I can just make out a familiar lollipop-shaped dock a short distance up the shore. I point to it. "That's my aunt's place. We can go there. There's a shallow beach and some first aid stuff inside if we need it."

Ben doesn't argue. Hell, this is turning out to be the easiest conversation we've ever had. By a kilometre!

Still clinging to each other like a pair of staticky, mismatched socks, we amble slowly toward Aunt Su's. A question occurs to me.

"So, what exactly are you doing out here, anyway?" I ask.

"Looking for you."

Wait a second. Isn't that supposed to be my answer? I waggle my head back and forth, trying to shake off the last of the spinning. It seems to work. I hold up a hand. "Thanks for all your help, Ben. I can walk fine now."

But he doesn't let go. And I don't try to make him. We're just a few metres away from the water. I can practically taste the lake in my mouth.

"I went by McCool's and saw Jake Hudson in your crappy little cubicle."

Silence.

"Why'd you quit?"

Long pause.

"Guess I decided my character was built enough."

More mysteries. I don't like that answer. "No, really."

But before he has the chance to say anything else about it, we're at Aunt Su's dock. Ben leads me down the beach, straight to the water. He must be pretty freaked out about my injured hands because we don't even stop to take off our shoes. The next thing I know, we're walking into the lake. It's so cold. My skin breaks out in an instant rash of goosebumps. Every instinct in my body is telling me to stop walking, go back, dry off, warm up. But still, I let him lead me further into the water. As soon as we're waist deep, Ben takes my hands and plunges them under the surface. He swishes his hands over mine, oh-so-carefully extracting stones and cleaning out the wounds. It hurts a bit, but I let him do the job. When my hands come up a minute later, the stones are gone. And from what I can see through the darkness, the bleeding has stopped.

"How do you feel?"

I force out a shaky smile. "Thanks. I think I'm fine now."

"Still ..."

He keeps a tight hold on my hands. There's no way in hell he's letting go yet. Believe you me. And I know it has nothing to do with applying pressure to the cuts.

"Lily, I did some more reading on the sleep thing yesterday ..."

I nod. The pain in my hands seems to be travelling to my chest.

"Do you know you'll die if you don't sleep?"

Another nod. And then I have to close my eyes before he can see the tears.

"I'm not going to let that happen to you, Lily," he whispers. "We'll figure out how to get your sleep back. I promise." His words make an echo over the water ... over my ears ... through my insides and back out again. Suddenly, a tall wave comes up behind me and nudges us closer. My eyes flutter open just in time to see Ben leaning his head down towards mine. I feel my heart pick up speed. Above us, the half moon peeks out from behind the clouds to watch what's about to happen.

"Ben ..."

"Lily ..."

My face is in his eyes. *No, don't fall in love with him,* warns the nasty little voice in my head. *What's the point when you're going to be dead any minute now?*

"I think I still have your jean jacket."

"Keep it."

I can hear his breaths getting closer as he slowly leans his head the rest of the way. My eyes drift closed. One of Ben's hands falls on my cheek. And then his kiss on my lips. It's like a feather sweeping over my mouth. It's like Niagara Falls crashing over my head. Everything starts to spin again. My knees wobble. I grab on to his arms to keep myself from tumbling into the lake. His kiss tastes like Froot Loops. No, better than that. His kiss tastes like the circle of milk in the bottom of the bowl after the Froot Loops are gone. No, better than that.

Pink, sweet, warm, delicious. Perfect.

Silver waves rise up around us. His hand curves into the small of my back. My fingers climb up to find the soft curls at the nape of his neck. The bottom of the lake disappears and suddenly I'm floating. We're floating. Together.

Oh my God!

So, yeah. Now I understand what all the fuss is about.

TWENTY

I guess perfection can never last long, can it? After lending us twenty minutes of awesome, the lake decided to shoo us away. The water was so cold it had sucked practically every molecule of warmth from our bodies. And as you can imagine, blue lips aren't much good for kissing. Or talking, for that matter.

"I think w-we better head b-back," Ben says, lifting himself out of the kiss. I nod, too cold to speak. We're both shaking like a pair of human earthquakes by the time we make it to the shore. I point to my aunt's little weather-beaten cabin, glowing grey in the darkness. "L-let's g-g-go inside and d-dry off," I somehow manage to say between teeth clatters. My jaw sounds just like Aunt Su's old manual typewriter when she used to be on a story bender. Wild!

"S-so this is y-your aunt's c-c-c-cabin?" Ben asks. His hands reach out to feel the wood. His eyes sweep over the structure.

"C-c-can you help fix it?"

He nods. "Sure I c-c-can. D-do you have a k-key?"

"I'll g-go g-get it. B-be right back."

Hugging my arms to my chest, I bound up the beach to get the key from inside the gnome. On the way, I pass Aunt Su's herb garden and nearly trip over a new patch of black-eyed Susans that must have sprung up since my last visit. As I scramble to find my balance, my mind flies back to a warm day last June when Aunt Su and I planted the seeds. "Can't wait for these to come up. They're one of my most favourite flowers," she said, pointing to the spot right next to the flagstone path where she wanted me to dig. I remember being surprised by that. "They are?" I asked, putting down the shovel to check the photo on the seed pack. *How had I not known that?* The flowers in the picture were bright yellow — not purple, her usual favourite. She smiled as she scattered the seeds gently into the dirt. "Well, we share the same name, don't we?" I remember being totally shocked at that. Aunt Su was named after a flower too? "And these Susans will grow to be strong, proud, and a little bit wild — just like me." She leaned back on her heels and clapped the dirt from her palms. "They'll come up when they're good and ready — probably in the fall." Then she reached to take my hands in hers. "They're going to keep this garden alive when everything else around is long gone."

I remember at the time having the distinct feeling that she wasn't talking about flowers anymore.

I lean down and let my fingers brush over the soft yellow petals. Aunt Su was right: this little plant is the only thing left in bloom on the property. For a moment, I almost forget about my shivering body. But then a breeze blows in off the lake and my jaw is seized with a fresh round of teeth chatters. I drop the flower and rush off to get the gnome. When I reach the porch, I turn around to look at Ben one more time. Just to be sure I haven't been, you know, hallucinating the whole thing. Against the backdrop of the morning sky, his tall body is a long shadow beside the wide, swaying lake. But he's definitely there. No hallucination.

Sigh.

That's when I see it happen. He doesn't know I'm looking, but I see the whole thing. With one fluid movement, Shadowy Ben lifts the silver chain off his neck and hurls it into the lake. The metal of the initial ring flashes briefly in the moonlight before hitting the surface with a minuscule splash and disappearing under the dark waves. Shocked, I scamper off to get the key before he can catch me spying. By the time I pull it out of the gnome, Ben's waiting for me by the back door of the cabin. Somehow he looks different without the necklace. For one thing, he's smiling.

I unlock the door and we drip over the threshold into the main room. Both of us are soaked through to our bones. I shiver as we stand there in the middle of Aunt Su's stuff. My thoughts are feeling strangely sluggish and slow, like they're wading through a giant jar of strawberry jam. I turn to look at Ben for direction. *What now?*

"We really should take care of those scrapes on your hands."

Okay, yeah, that sounds logical.

I lift my trembling arm and wave at the door beside us. "First aid kit's in the bathroom. Under the sink."

Ben disappears into Aunt Su's little bathroom and comes out a few seconds later with an armful of green towels and a small white box. He kneels beside me, dries off my hands, and covers up my shredded palms with a triple layer of gauze bandages.

"Okay, next thing: we have to get warm," Ben says, rising to his feet. He hands me one of the towels and wraps the other around his shoulders. "I think it'd be good if we could change into something dry. Any clothes here we can borrow?"

Yup, another good idea.

"First door on the left," I reply, pointing a shaky blue fingertip. "Check the bottom drawer of the dresser."

He comes back a minute later with one of Aunt Su's faded

purple T-shirts in one hand and an old, fuzzy wool blanket in the other. He hands the T-shirt to me.

I shiver and take it. "But what are you going to wear?"

That seems to amuse him. "Your aunt and I aren't exactly the same size," Ben says, holding up the blanket. "Don't worry, I'll be fine with this."

And so, in the dim moonlight that's spilling through the lake-side window, we towel our dripping bodies off and strip down to our underwear. Then we hang our wet stuff up to dry on Aunt Su's rusty old laundry room clothes horse. I try really, really hard not to fixate too long on the sight of Ben standing beside me in his wet boxer shorts. But it isn't easy. The body I've only been able to see in my imagination is suddenly there in front of me in all its holy awesomeness. Even though my brain is still stuck in slo-mo, my heart is knocking wildly against my ribs. I can feel the pounding all the way up to my ears. It sounds almost the same as General MacArthur's frantic shoe-tapping on the floor. Eventually, when Ben notices me noticing him, I turn away and pull the purple T-shirt over my head. Slowly, to give my cheeks a chance to turn back to their natural colour. As the shirt comes down across my nose, the smell of Aunt Su brings an avalanche of old memories crashing along with it. Just like that night in the mint patch. Only for some reason, this time the memories are coming to me through a thick layer of Fluffernutter. Weird. Maybe that's why I'm able to hold back the flood of tears. They're sticking to the fluff. By the time my face pops out of the neck hole, the sting behind my lids has disappeared.

My eyes find Ben. He's staring at me with a funny look on his face — like I'm some bizarre experimental art installation that doesn't make any kind of sense. "Sure you're okay?"

Nod.

"Why don't we rest here for a bit? I'm guessing you're not up for the walk home yet, are you?"

Shake.

"The sun'll be rising in a couple of hours. We can hang out here and wait for the light."

Another nod. Trust me, when your brain feels like a squishy bowl of oatmeal, you'll agree with pretty much anything. By this point, I've completely lost all track of time. And most of my senses too. What on earth is wrong with me? Am I suffering from hypothermia? Love sickness? Symptoms of imminent death by exhaustion? A panicked shiver suddenly passes over my skin. Yeah, that last one is probably right.

Ben pulls the old quilt off the couch and stretches it out on the floor next to the giant window. We lie down side by side on the quilt and he pulls the woolly blanket up over us. I huddle next to him for warmth. He huddles back. The shivering is starting to ease off a little bit. The moon is still watching us from out on the water. I can see the waves rolling up the beach. And sliding back down again. One by one. In … out … in … out …

Hypnotic. My body's a helium balloon. A big, silvery blue one. Floating higher and higher …

"Is your Mom going to be worried about you?" Ben asks, breaking through my trance.

I take a few extra seconds to process the question through my sludgy brain.

"No, she thinks I'm sleepin' at Emmasouse."

"Emma's house?"

Nod.

"What's wrong with your voice?"

It's the slurred speech of the terminally sleepless, the voice in my head calls out. But I don't want to scare him with the truth. "Jus coldlips," is what I say instead.

"Okay." Ben huddles me closer.

"What abouchor Dad?" I ask.

"No. He definitely won't notice I'm gone."

"What'see like?" I really just want to get him talking so I won't have to. I'm so fuzzy-brained. It's like a giant sheep is sitting on my head.

"My dad?" Kilometre-long pause here. "Defeated. That's what he's like."

"Huh?"

"Like I told you, it's a long story."

"S'okay. I wannahearit."

He doesn't speak for a full minute. And when he does, his voice is hard as a giant block of concrete. "When the economy collapsed, my dad's construction business kind of collapsed along with it. He lost it all. There was literally nothing left. Not enough to keep our home. Or our cars. Not even enough to pay my school tuition. Even my university savings were gone. My mother bailed and ran off with her new rich boyfriend. Everything we had in the city got auctioned off and we moved up here."

Everything they owned gone? Just like that? No home, no savings, no company left for Ben to take over one day? I don't know what to say. So instead, I just huddle a bit closer.

"I haven't told anyone this, but it's gotten really bad, Lily," Ben continues. His block of concrete voice has suddenly shrunk down to small bag of pebbles. "After we got here, Dad had to take a second mortgage on the cottage. And right now we can't even afford the property taxes on the place, let alone the payments. Dad's ... well, he's having a hard time dealing with it. He won't even get out of bed to look for work. I'm all he's got. It's all up to me, now."

Ben's eyes drop away from mine. He starts twisting little fluff balls off the woolly blanket. "I sort of lied about the whole 'character-building' thing," he says. "Truth is, I took the job because we need the money. Badly."

Something about this whole thing isn't making sense. Even in my fuzzy-minded state, I can tell there's a little piece of his mystery still missing. "So whydjoo quit McCool's then?"

"Had to. I knew there was no way I'd ever get through the school year half asleep. If they fail me, I'll never get into university. Better just to take some time away from school until I can concentrate on my marks again. I was trying to find you and let you know."

I can't believe what I'm hearing. *Oh my God — Ben's quitting school?*

"You can't ..."

He holds up a hand to stop me. "Yes, I can, Lily. I have to. We need money. I need a job that's more of a nine-to-five thing. Plus, someone's got to be around at night to keep an eye on Dad."

I'm quiet for a minute, trying to take all this new information in through my Jell-O brain. Ben's quitting school. His family's in trouble. They're running out of money. I glance down at the dollar store D'watch on his wrist and suddenly understand what happened to his other watch. And his iPod. And his leather jacket. *Merde*, this is brutal! He's gone from big-city-private-school-golden-boy to penniless-sleep-deprived-small-town-dropout in less than a year. No wonder he's grumpy! I can't believe he's been listening to all my problems while he's dealing with this behind the scenes! What if they have to sell their house? What if they have to move away from Big Bend? Would he move to Vancouver to be with his mom? And then I remember about the necklace. The one expensive thing it seems he didn't pawn.

"Whooz SB?"

"What?"

"Th'ring. Sit your mom's?"

"The ring? No, it's definitely not my mom's."

"So?"

Long pause. "The B is for my name and the S is the initial of a girl from my old school. Savannah Lawrence."

My heart flatlines. "Girlfriend?"

"Ex, actually."

Savannah. A girl with that name is all fake suntanned skin and blond flowy hair. I hate her instantly. I nudge Ben's ribs for more information. "So?"

"So we were together just over a year. The whole thing was like a two-way addiction. We couldn't get enough of each other. I gave her the ring on our first anniversary. I had it made with both our initials — like we'd be together forever. I thought I was in love."

"Love?" The word drops out of my mouth like a toad. I so badly want to track Savannah Lawrence down and pull every strand of her blond hair out of her head. "So wahappened?

Ben tilts his head back and groans. "Man, I was *such* an idiot. Savannah broke it off the minute she found out Dad went bust. She didn't even do it in person. There was a note and the ring waiting for me on the front porch of my house when I got home from school."

"Oh, Ben ..." Crap. What else is there to say?

"Yeah, I was a wreck. And then the next day, Mom left."

Quelles maudite salopes. "So whydjoo keep th'ring?"

His eyes meet mine. "To remind me not to trust anyone again. Especially not another pretty girl."

Pretty girl? My core body temperature instantly shoots up ten degrees.

"So whydjoo throw it away?"

Long pause. "I don't need it anymore."

My heart does a little somersault. I so badly want to say some-thing here. Something to let him know how much I care about him. Like how speaking his name out loud makes me feel like I'm singing in a choir. Or how looking at his face gives me a glimmer of hope that I might not actually die a horrible, premature death. And how, for reasons I don't even fully understand, thinking about him is the one and only thing that's getting me through the long, ugly nights. Maybe even the only thing that's been keeping me alive this long. But I can't get a sound out. My voice is officially kaput. So I Morse-code eyelid blink him instead. *You can trust me, Ben ... I wouldn't ever hurt you.*

He puts his arms around me and pulls me even closer. I think I hear him whisper, "I know." Or maybe it's just a hallucination. A second later, his hand is on my face, brushing straggly damp strands of hair out of my eyes. "Close your eyes now, Lily. You need some rest." I take a long, deep breath. He smells like the lake. Like our kiss. My head swims at the thought of it. I let the breath out slowly. It feels good to be here with him. *So* good. I've been spending so much time pushing people out of my life, I never imagined how nice it would feel to let someone in. Just like Aunt Su said in her note.

I think she'd be proud if she could see me now.

If people were fonts, Ben would be ... Ben would be ...

Ben isn't a font.

I put my cheek on his shoulder and close my eyes. His fingers oh-so gently brush over the mess of my wet hair. For the first time in forever, I feel genuinely happy. I want to bring my face to his and kiss him until the sun comes up. But my head is too heavy to move; it feels like it weighs a bazillion pounds. I want to run my hands all over his body and learn all its measurements and angles and calculate how they'd fit with mine. But my hands are sinking in quicksand. And the rest of me is following fast. My breath is whispering in and out of me so slow ... so slow ... like the baby waves that inch up and down the sand at low tide.

This is it. It's all ending here. In Ben's arms.

Not such a bad way to go.

Funny, I thought I'd be petrified when this moment finally came. But I'm not at all. I'm totally and completely at peace. And I feel my muscles go limp. And I sense everything go dark as death comes to take me away.

See you in the Guinness book!

TWENTY-ONE

September 21st

Okay, so I'm not dead. But you probably figured that out already, didn't you? 'Cause if I was really dead, this would be an epilogue, not a chapter, right?

Right.

So if I'm not dead, what the hell happened? I open my eyes to see the sun misting through the giant window beside me. *Hey, how'd I miss the sunrise?* I peer around. There's the lake, slapping against the sand. There's the creaky old glider swinging in the breeze on the porch. There's Aunt Su's tattered and woolly blanket pulled up high and flopped over my ear. And ... jeepers creepers! There's Ben beside me, head propped up on the palm of his hand, staring down at me like a Greek god. His face brightens when my eyes connect with his.

"Hey."

"Hey."

I lift my head carefully. The sheep has somehow miraculously lifted off my brain. Bits and pieces from the night before are slowly coming back to me. Emma's house ... the chase in the dark that didn't happen ... the kiss in the lake that did. That's when I notice Ben is wearing his clothes again, although they're still a bit damp-looking and wrinkly from our late-night swim.

I glance quickly down at myself: I'm still wearing Aunt Su's T-shirt.

"So, anyone ever tell you that you snore when you sleep?" he says.

Excuse me? I yank the blanket off my ear and sit up straight. "What did you just say?"

"I said that you snore."

"No, the other thing. The sleeping part."

"Yeah, right. Didn't you say you were having problems with that?"

"I am!"

He takes my hand. His face stretches into a deliriously happy grin. Another first. "Could've fooled me," he says. The dimple in his chin winks at me. I stare at him in shock. Does that mean I slept? I think it does! Oh my God! *I slept!* I'm not going to die a hideously premature death after all! It's like a miracle! For Pete's sake, I totally feel like Ebenezer Scrooge waking up on Christmas morning with a new chance at life! I fling off the blanket and leap to my feet. Energy is vibrating through my arms and legs like a symphony. My fists pump in the air and I spin around in a happy pirouette.

"I slept! Ben! Ben! I got my sleep back!!"

I lean down, throw my arms around his neck and tackle him to the floor. I haven't felt this good in weeks. "I'm not going to die! I'm not going to die!" I say, hugging him so hard it hurts. "Thank you. Thank you for helping me get my sleep back."

"You're welcome — *ow!* — I think." He's pretending to be hurt but I can hear the smile in his voice. So I hug him even harder. "Oof ... Isn't it a little early in the afternoon for wrestling?"

I stop squeezing. Afternoon? Uh-oh. I look down at my bare wrist. No watch. "What time is it?"

Ben stretches out a long arm and points to the purple cuckoo clock on the wall beside the kitchen. "Just past twelve-thirty."

I jump to my feet. "*Merde!*"

"What?"

"My parents! I better get home before Emma reports me AWOL!"

As if on cue, there's a sudden pounding at the cabin door. And then a bellow so loud, it rattles the creaky old walls. "Lily MacArthur? Are you in there?"

My eyes reach for Ben. "That's my dad. Guess I've been reported."

Pound-pound-pound. The wooden door heaves like it's going to split in half.

"*LILY?*"

The bellow has officially erupted into a scream. I jump to my feet and dash to the laundry room for my clothes. "Yeah, Dad. I'm here. Just gimme a sec."

A moment later, dressed in little Swartz sister's damp skinny jeans and T-shirt, I swing open the door. Dad glares down at me. His eyes are thunderclouds and his nostrils are flaring like an angry bull. I can't remember a time I've ever seen him so mad.

"Where have you been?" he howls. The Tabasco sauce on his breath gusts into my face. He must have OD'd on it at breakfast this morning. Too much of the stuff always brings out his temper.

"Calm down, Dad ..."

"Don't you tell me to calm down, missy! Your friend Emma called and said you ran away from her house last night." Muscling past me, he marches straight into the cabin. "We've been worried sick! Emma's been crying all morning."

"She has?" Ugh, poor Emma. She's the first real friend I've ever had. Sleep-deprived paranoia or not, I shouldn't have bailed on her like that. I make a mental note to call her later and apologize.

"Yes, she has!" he yells. "And your poor mother's a hysterical mess. She was even too upset to come out and look for you. You

know, she's positive you fell in the lake and drowned." Dad stops
in his tracks the instant he spots Ben. Ben who's standing by the
window folding up the quilt into a giant slippery square. Well,
hexagon, actually.

"Who the hell are *you*?"

Nice, Dad! I hop over to the window and grab the quilt from
Ben's hands. Why can't anybody with a Y chromosome fold linens
neatly? "Dad. This is Ben Matthews."

"Was this all about a boy?" His big hand flies up and slaps his
forehead. "God! What's gotten into you, Lily? I can't believe it."
Dad's anger is quickly dissolving into that classic look of paternal
pain — you know, the one that strikes the moment fathers inevitably wake up to the realization their daughters are growing up.
He clutches at his heart and staggers slightly to the left. "Is *he* the
reason you ran away?"

"No ... Well ... Oh, come on, Dad! Don't be so melodramatic!"

He jabs a sausagey finger in Ben's direction. I swear he looks
like he's millimetres away from taking a swing at him. "What did
you say your last name was, kid?"

"Matthews. Ben Matthews."

And then the strangest thing happens. In a flash of a second,
Dad's anger seems to melt away to nothingness. It's like magic.
The lines in his forehead smooth out, his eyes soften, and his
nostrils shrink back down to normal.

"Not Steven Matthews' kid?"

"Yeah, that's right."

His jabbing finger falls down to his side. With a nod of his
head, Dad lets go of his heart, steps toward Ben, and holds out
his right hand. "Well, it's nice to finally meet you, son. I've known
your father for years."

Okay ... what the hell is going on here?

"Yeah ... nice to meet you too, Mr. MacArthur."

I watch them shake hands. Dad and Ben. My father and the guy I'm crazy over the moon for. I should feel happy about this, right? So why does it feel like my stomach has swallowed every single one of my vital organs? And why do my legs suddenly feel like a pair of overcooked linguini noodles? I take a small step back and sink down onto the couch. The cushions sag heavily to the left as Dad sinks down beside me.

Maybe he senses a "MacArthur family talk" coming on, because Ben throws me a little wink and reaches his hand out in the air. "I think I should be going now, Lily. I better get home and let my dad know I'm okay. See you around."

I jump to my feet to stop him. *No, don't leave yet! There's so much more I want to tell you. Like how much I like you. And how much Aunt Su would have liked you. And how now I know the answer to my missing sleep was with you all this time. And how grateful I am that you helped me last night. And how desperately I want to help you now. And … and …*

My mouth tumbles open but no words come out. There are way too many and they all stick in my throat. Too late anyway, because before I know it, Ben's gone. I listen to the sound of his shoes scrunching down the driveway. When I know for sure he's out of earshot, I plunk back down onto the sofa and swivel around to face Dad.

"Mind telling me what just happened there?"

He frowns. "Aren't I supposed to be asking you that question?"

I poke him with my elbow. "I mean it, Dad. How do you know Ben's father?"

Pause. Deep breath in. Long gust of Tabasco out.

"Steven Matthews is … well, *was* one of our biggest donors. Every year when he arrived in Big Bend for the season, he would come into my office, sit for a cup of coffee, and cut me a substantial cheque for the charity. And it wasn't just a tax deduction for him — he honestly cared about how the money was going to be used. And who it was going to help. He's really one of the most generous, down-to-earth people I've had the pleasure of knowing."

I swallow hard, trying to push down the prickly little lump that's suddenly stuck in the middle of my throat. "Ben told me they're broke now. Is that true?"

Dad shakes his head slowly. "It's true. Poor Steve definitely didn't deserve what happened. I mean, not only did he lose everything he'd ever worked for, but then his wife left him. I think I heard she's living out west now."

"Vancouver, actually."

"Okay, Vancouver." Dad rakes a hand through his thick, black hair. "And from what I've heard around town, Steve's pretty much at the end of his rope. Apparently, he's been drinking. Rather heavily, I gather. I've tried dropping in to see him once or twice, but he won't answer the door." He takes my hand and gives it a tight squeeze. "Your friend Ben must be having a really hard time right now. It's good to know he's got you to talk to."

Before I can say anything, the pocket of Dad's jeans start to ring. "Bloody hell. It's your mother." He pulls out his cell and brings it to his ear. "Lis? Yeah, I found her ... She's fine ... I will ... Okay." He closes it with a slap and tosses it down onto the back of Aunt Su's black rhino carving. I mean, *my* black rhino carving.

"She mad?" I ask, smoothing out the deep pattern of lake wrinkles still creasing my damp, borrowed clothes.

"She'll be fine. We'll give her a few minutes to calm down before we take you home." He puts an arm around my shoulder and pulls me close. And that's when he notices my soggy little wardrobe malfunction. "For Christ's sake, whose clothes are you wearing? And why are they wet?" He leans down and gives me a sniff. "Jesus, Lily. *Did* you fall in the lake?"

I decide to plead the fifth on that one and change the subject. "You know, Dad, it's getting harder all the time to deal with Mom's shtick."

He laughs at that. "You're preaching to the choir, Sweetness."

"No, really. She actually had a lock installed on my window and door. Did you know that?"

"Lily ..."

"And she's talking about having this place condemned. Did you know *that*?"

"Lily ..."

"I can't take it anymore. I'm serious, her control issues are taking over my life!"

"Lily ..."

"You remember what it's like to be a teenager, don't you, Dad? 'Cause I don't think she does at all. And I need a bit of space to make my own mistakes. It's the only way I'm going to grow up."

"I know that."

"So would you tell *her*, please?"

"Yes, I'll talk to her. But just keep in mind, she's trying her best. She really is."

I have nothing to say to that. The purple cuckoo clock tick-tocks through the long, heavy silence.

After a few minutes, Dad speaks again. But this time, he definitely isn't laughing. "I think there's something you should know, Lily. Something about your mom. There's actually a very good reason why she is the way she is. I know she's never told you — she probably never will. But you really need to hear it. And this feels like the right time."

My stomach muscles tense up into a giant fist. *Oh man, not another secret!* Lately, my life feels like it's coming straight out of a paperback mystery novel. Catching Dad's dark eyes with mine,

I lean in close and whisper: "She's not my real mother, is she?" *Because that would actually explain a lot,* the little Aunt Su voice in my head adds silently.

Dad's mouth falls open in shock. "Lily Rose MacArthur! Where did that come from? Of course she's your real mother."

"Okay then, is she wanted by the police or something?"

He rolls his eyes just like an irritated school kid. "Oh for Christ's sake, would you just let me tell you, already?"

"Fine, sorry. Go ahead." *Where exactly is he going with this?*

"You've heard there was a drowning in the lake when your mother was little?"

"Yeah. That's why she made me wear water wings until I was twelve."

"Right. Well, what you don't know is that it was your grandfather who drowned."

"My grandfather? As in, Mom's dad?"

"That's right. Su's dad too, of course."

I shake my head. "I knew he died a long time ago ... but how come nobody told me he drowned in the lake?"

"It's just not something your mother or Su liked to talk about. His death really devastated them both. In some ways, I think it changed them forever."

"Changed them how?"

"Su was older when it happened — almost thirty. She took her father's death as a lesson: life is short and you'd better make the most of the time you've got. A few days after the funeral, she quit her job at Beachside Books and started writing her first novel."

Beachside Books? Guess that's where she met Mr. Swartz.

"And Mom?"

"Your mother was only a little girl when her father drowned. The way she coped was to clutch on tightly to everyone else she ever loved. To keep them close and safe." A hint of a shadow passes over Dad's face as he speaks.

"And I'm guessing you're speaking from personal experience?"

His answer comes out in slo-mo, like he's choosing his words very carefully. "As you can imagine, it wasn't easy being married to someone like your mom."

Oh, man. My poor suffocated dad.

"And Lily," he continues after a long pause. "You must know that there's no one in this world your mother loves more than you."

The prickly little lump is suddenly back in my throat — bigger than a tennis ball this time. I gulp it down, along with a budding crop of hot tears. "All right, I get what you're saying here, but she's got to let go a bit or I'll go insane." Then I close my eyes and finally speak the secret wish that's been living inside me for as long as I can remember. "Please don't ever tell her I said this, but I always wished Aunt Su was my real mother." It feels good to release those awful words. Even if the sound of them makes me feel truly ugly for the first time in my life.

Dad pats my hand. "This might surprise you, Sweetness, but I think your mom always secretly wanted to be more like her sister. You know, she was intensely jealous of her."

My eyes fly open again. "Of Aunt Su?"

Nod. Dad's hand-patting picks up speed.

"But how is that even possible? What did she have that Mom didn't?"

His dark eyebrows bounce with surprise. "You, of course."

Merde. I lean back on the couch and let out a long, deep breath. Suddenly, I'm so tired I just want to curl back up and go to sleep all over again. So tired, I almost break down and tell him about Aunt Su's letter and the truth about how she really died. Almost. It's on the tip of my tongue. But I don't. It's not my truth to tell. So I take another long, deep breath. "I just need some space, Dad

… you know?"

He leans forward and sighs. Pokey elbows jutting into big, thick knees. "Maybe you and your mom would have the chance to be closer if you didn't have to live together all the time. I could talk to her about the idea of you coming to stay with me for a while. If you'd want to, that is."

Just the thought of it makes me want to break into a little happy dance. *Yes, I want. I definitely want!* I sit back up again. "But do you really think she'd go for it?"

"Worth a try, isn't it?"

"Where would my space be, though? Your apartment is so small."

"Yeah, well, I have a feeling we might just be able to afford a bigger place now." He pulls out a crumpled envelope from his jeans pocket and hands it to me. Am I imagining it, or is his hand shaking?

"This came in the mail yesterday. It's all yours, Sweetness."

"What is it?" I ask, running my fingertips over the little red drips of Tabasco sauce dotting the smooth, white paper. At the top left corner of the envelope is the name *Colville Press* followed by an address I've never heard of in New York City. The words "The estate of Shoshanah M. Chase" are very officially printed across the middle. My stomach flip-flops.

Dad nudges me with his elbow. "Go ahead — open it up."

I shake my head. Hard. Really, just about the last thing I want to do right now is open another mysterious letter about Aunt Su. "Maybe you should just tell me, Dad. What is it?"

He puts a trembly hand on my knee, as if to steady us both. "It's a royalty cheque for Su's books. I spoke to Mr. Duffy about it. He says we can expect one of these to come in the mail about every six months."

A royalty cheque? I reach in and pull out a long slip of turquoise paper. It has my name printed right there on the front. And Dad's name right underneath.

Arial Narrow. *Nice!*

And underneath our names is a string of digits so long, it's hard even for me — the enriched math genius — to take it all in. A number way bigger than the amount of hours you'll be sleeping away during your life.

Three hundred and twenty-four thousand, seven hundred eighty-six dollars and fifty-two cents.

The cheque flutters down to the dusty cabin floor.

Sacre bleu!

It's a bequeathing fortune.

TWENTY-TWO

Right. So, Aunt Su was totally, completely mind-bendingly loaded. Turns out the rights for all those cheap, trashy romance novels are worth a veritable fortune. And on top of that, she was a closet real estate mogul. In other words, I didn't just inherit a rundown little cabin with a hairy garden gnome out front and a rusty moped in the garage. Oh no. I inherited a giant chunk of premium lakeside property that stretches for kilometres in every direction. According to Mr. Duffy, Aunt Su bought it all up piece by piece over the years. She was so desperate for privacy that every time she sold a new book, she bought herself another chunk of land. A massive real estate bubble of personal space. Which, by the way, totally explained why she didn't have any neighbours. Aunt Su owned half of Big Bend's lakefront.

Which means, of course, that now *I* own half of Big Bend's lakefront.

Head between knees. Deep breath in ... deep breath out ...

Okay, I'm all right now. Yeah, as you can guess, I really didn't see this coming! But can you blame me? It was all so easy to miss. Aunt Su never lived the lifestyle of the rich and famous. I don't ever remember her talking about money or wanting to buy a fancy car or go shopping on the French Riviera. She never wore jewellery or fancy clothes. As far as I know, she didn't like polo or caviar or golf.

Her writing, the lake, me. Those were the things she got the most joy from. And none of them cost a penny.

Quel irony.

Dad said I'll get access to the money and properties when I turn eighteen. He'll help me decide what to do with all of it at that point. "Until then, I'm going to have to approve any purchases you want to make, since I'm the executor. Okay, Sweetness?"

"Yup, fine with me."

And it really is fine with me. Fact is, now that I have my sleep back again, there are only a few things I can think of that I want in life, and money isn't going to help me with any of them.

To start with, I want my freedom. After our talk, Dad got right on the phone and started the parental negotiations with Mom. He knows how to handle her better than anyone else. In the end, she agreed to let me live with Dad for the rest of the school year as long as I come to stay with her on weekends. Dad and I are going to start looking for a new apartment together this week. Really hoping Dad's right — that Mom and I will get closer with a bit of distance. It's all so ingeniously oxymoronic, it *has* to work. Dontcha think?

The other thing I want to do is figure out the final place for Aunt Su's ashes. I got a good idea that last night at the cabin with Ben. But, believe it or not, the only person in the world who can help me make the idea work is none other than Todd Nelson. First thing after breakfast, I walk over to his house — which, incidentally, looks way nicer without the sprinkling of wrecked kids all over the property. Todd's on the front lawn with what looks to be his grandfather, raking leaves into neat little piles. If I didn't know better, I'd almost think they were sorting the piles according to shape and colour of leaf. I have to resist the

urge to jump in and scatter them to the wind. Todd would probably forgive me but his grandpa looks pretty harsh — like he might
even have less of a sense of humour than General MacArthur.
If that's even humanly possible.

"Hey, Todd," I say, hovering back on the edge of the driveway.
He drops his rake when he sees me.

"Lily?" He glances over at his grandpa, and when he turns
back to me, I see his face is brighter than the pile of red maple
leaves at his feet. "What are you doing here?"

Stepping over the leaves, he strides over to where I'm standing.
His grandpa has his arms propped up on the end of the rake
handle. He's watching us with an overabundance of interest.

"I think we should talk," I say, lowering my voice to a whisper
so his grandpa won't overhear. "First of all, I want to say that I
think you're really nice. And smart. And it was sweet of you to
try and help me out last week in the hallway." A slow smile starts
to build on Todd's lips. I hurry to finish my point before it takes
over his face. "But ... well, I'm so sorry ... but I just don't like you
that way. You know what I mean, right?"

In a flash, his smile disintegrates. *Okay, yeah, he knows what
I mean.* Todd's face is burning so bright red, I worry it might just
implode. He shuffles his feet and shoves his hands in his hoodie
pockets. "But what about the night of the party ... What about
what happened —"

I hold up a hand to stop him from saying any more. Now my
face is burning too. "No. I was drunk, Todd. I wasn't acting like
myself. I ... it's ... I wouldn't want that to happen again."

He lowers his eyes to the ground. *Zut.* I've hurt his feelings.
I take a step closer and give him a buddy-like punch in the arm.
Hard, but not hard enough to hurt. "I'd really like to be friends,
though — if you want."

When he speaks again, his voice is a low rumble. "Emma told

me you don't have any friends. Well, except for her."

"Yeah, well … guess you could say I'm turning over a new leaf," I say. My introverted self lets out a weak squeal of protest. I ignore it, reach down, grab a handful from the neatly raked pile at my feet and toss them at his head. Leaves scatter around us like confetti. By the time they've landed, Todd's smiling again. For all the right reasons, now. Behind him, I see his grandfather scowl and pick up his rake. "So, what do you say?" I ask.

He buddy-punches me back. Hard, but not quite hard enough to hurt. "Okay. We can be friends. Guess I'll take what I can get."

See, Lily? That wasn't so hard, the little voice in my head says.

I let out a shaky breath. "If it's okay, I have a favour to ask you." Once I explain what I need, Todd happily abandons his raking and takes me on a shopping trip. To his family's garden centre.

━◆━

And of course, the other thing I want is to help Ben. And fast. Before he makes the biggest mistake of his life and drops out of school. I wiggle-wormed his address out of Dad and head over there first thing the next morning. The Matthews' home is a large, rust-red cottage in the newer, more touristy part of the lakefront. It's the kind of place that pretends to be quaint and country-ish on the outside but in reality is the exact opposite. From the two-car garage and the landscaped front yard, it isn't hard to imagine there's probably a lap pool and a perfectly matched quaint red boathouse somewhere out back.

I walk up to the front stoop and reach for the doorbell. But my finger freezes in midair as I notice the yellow piece of paper tacked to the outside of the red wooden door. I lean in to read it. My stomach drops to the ground the instant I take in the ugly black words crawling across the top of the page.

Notice of Foreclosure.

TWENTY-THREE

I pound on the door. The ugly yellow sign shakes with the force of my fist.

What does this mean? Is Ben still here, or have he and his dad been kicked out already?

My mind spins with images of Homeless Ben wandering the streets, busking for spare change, digging through trashcans for scraps of food. Ben and his father, dirty and thin, curled up inside a pair of tattered sleeping bags as they pass night after night on the beach. I pound on the door again, louder this time. The date stamped across the top of the letter jumps out at me. September 16. Last Monday — the day before Ben had his angry meltdown in the hallway. Three days before he quit school and ditched his job at McCool Fries. My head spins even faster as all the awful dots start connecting together in my brain. A few seconds later, the door swings open. It's him. I have to bite my lower lip to stop from crying with relief. He's wearing a faded pair of jeans and an old U2 concert tee. And his hair's all tousled and messy. From sleep or a night full of tossing and turning? Jeepers creepers! I'm so happy to see him, I have to stop myself from hurling myself into his arms. My eyes drop down to my shoes.

"Ben," I say. Yeah, the Pop Rocks are still going strong.

"Hey."

I peek up around him and see big stacks of cardboard boxes littering the floor. *Merde*! I have to act fast!

"Can we talk for a minute?"

Ben glances over his shoulder. "Yeah, but my dad's not up yet," he says, stepping out onto the porch and pulling the door closed quietly behind him. "So it has to be out here."

His dad's sleeping ... or passed out drunk? I don't ask, 'cause I'm not sure I really want to know.

He puts a hand to his forehead, shielding his eyes from the bright sun shining behind me. "So, did your father calm down yet? He looked pretty wound up yesterday."

What's going on? He's getting kicked out of his home and he's asking about me?

I jab my finger against the yellow sign behind his head. "Mind telling me what this is about, Ben?"

He actually has the nerve to laugh. "Just a love letter from the bank."

Unbelievable.

"How can you joke around at a time like this? I mean, are they really going to take away your house? Where will you go?"

My voice is breaking to pieces over these words. I think Ben senses it because his lips press into a grimace and then all of a sudden, I see his carefully guarded walls come crashing down. No more mask of boredom. No more flippy jokes. Finally, he offers up a glimpse of his real feelings. And the pain I see in his eyes slices through me like a knife. His face crumples and he leans against the doorframe, like he's suddenly lost the energy to hold himself up.

"I've made a couple of calls. We've still got a few days to figure it out."

A couple of calls? That's it? Not exactly what I'd call a plan.

Reaching past him, I yank the paper off the door and scan my eyes down the page. It says the residence has to be vacated in ten days. I crush it between my fingers and let it fall to the ground. Time to get serious. I pull in a few deep breaths while my eyes fixate on Ben's hand — the one that seems to be saluting me. It looks strong but tired at the same time. And the healthy-looking suntan I'd noticed back on that first night we met has almost completely faded away to nothing. I want so badly to reach up and take that hand in mine. And then the other hand. And then wrap them both around me like the night in Aunt Su's cabin. I take a small step closer. Another breath — shuddery like wind blowing through a tunnel. My eyes float down to his face. *Zut*, why am I so nervous?

"Listen, I came here because ... well ... I don't even know where to start. This is going to sound really strange but," *another deep, calming breath*, "I came here because I, well I-I have a present for you."

His salute drops like a dead weight down to his side. "What?"

"Aunt Su's cabin. I'm giving it to you. Well, you and your dad, actually. You guys can have it for as long as you need it. Just give it back to me whenever you're done."

His eyes widen. "Lily, I —"

"No way!" I say, holding up my hands to stop him. "You're absolutely *not* allowed to say no to me this time!"

"It's just that —"

"No, Ben!" I squeeze my eyes closed and shake my head. I am *not* going to let him turn this down. "Unh-unh. This is something I have to do. And you have to let me do it. I know that little cabin isn't anywhere near as nice as what you're used to, but it's free. And once we fix it up, nobody's going to kick you out. There wouldn't be any mortgage payments or property taxes to worry about. And you wouldn't have to quit school and ... and I want to help."

I have to stop speaking. One more word and I'll collapse into pieces right then and there. I just know it. Ben stops speaking too. Maybe he's one word away from collapsing also. The birds chirp in the birch tree beside us. The silence between us grows and grows until it becomes a giant sinkhole. Another minute and it'll swallow both of us up.

"So?" I finally ask. "Are you going to say something?"

Ben shakes his head. His answer is a dry whisper. "Why does it always feel like you're trying to come to my rescue?"

I reach for his hand. "Can you give me one good reason why the hell a girl can't be the knight in shining armour once in a while?" I tilt my eyes up to his and give him my best badass face. At least it revives his smile.

"No, I can't." His face drifts down towards mine. "Which means that yes, I can."

Oxymoronic. Yeah, this is definitely going to work.

He pulls me close and I can feel his heartbeat thumping against my chest through the thin fabric of our T-shirts. Ben seals our deal with the world's most delicious kiss. His smooth lips slide like melted honey against mine. About a bazillion times better than soft-serve chocolate ice cream on a hot, summer day. When we finally come up for air, I open my eyes and drop my heels back down to earth. That's when I see it. The moon hanging out over the lake. It's only mid-morning, but there it is. A pale crescent swinging in the big blue sky.

Kind of like a smile from above — a crinkly, heartbreakingly familiar kind of smile.

I tilt my face up to heaven and smile back.

A Short and Final Note from Me

Ben called up some of his old builder friends and a week later we gave the cabin a Lily-style makeover. Which means we gave it just enough of an improvement to keep it looking like itself (only a little bit better) and stop it from getting condemned. Turns out, the big problem was a few beams of rotting wood along the side facing the lake. It took a whole day to replace those. And seal up the seams to keep the moisture out. And clear out some of the clutter and clean out the dust and grime on the floor and scrub away the mould from the walls. Now it's all ready for when Ben and his dad move in next week. But before that happens, we have to dig up what's left of the marijuana plants growing rampant throughout the garden. In their place, I want to plant the twenty-six lily bulbs Todd helped me pick out from his family's garden centre. According to Todd, this is the perfect time of year to plant them.

And, also according to Todd, ashes make the best fertilizer. Who'd have thought?

My dad and Emma and Ben and Todd and Mr. Swartz were all with me when I did it. Even General MacArthur insisted on being there for the moment. I'm sort of happy she was. Once we finished fixing the cabin up, she was quick to surrender the battle and call off her crazy condemning scheme. Which makes me really hope this distance thing is already starting to work. Got all my digits crossed on this one.

The old me never would have cried in front of so many people.

Deborah Kerbel

But I couldn't help letting out a few tears as I emptied Aunt Su's pomegranate jar over the lily bulbs and turned the soil over with a trowel. I know with all my heart that this is the right spot for Aunt Su to rest. When the lilies sprout up next spring, there'll be yellow, red, white, pink, orange ... and, of course, purple. All of them helping to keep her garden alive, just like the black-eyed Susans that'll be pushing up beside them. And just like the Susans, my lilies will grow up strong, proud ... and, yup, a little bit wild.

Huh.

Maybe, just maybe, I'm not a total oxymoron after all.

ACKNOWLEDGEMENTS

I'd like to thank the following people for their help with this book:

First and foremost, *mille mercis* to my editor and publisher, Barry Jowett, for his unflagging confidence in my writing, and to Cormorant Books president Marc Côté for his strong support. And to the rest of the incredible team at Dancing Cat Books — Meryl Howsam, Bryan Ibeas, Angel Guerra, Tannice Goddard, and Jennifer Gallant — thank you for helping me bring *Under the Moon* into the world.

Huge thanks to my brave crew of "first-draft readers" — Helaine Becker, Sharon Jones, Kim Pape-Green, and Suri Rosen — for cheering me on to the finish line.

Heartfelt thanks to Simone Spiegel for being such a wonderful sounding board and eagle-eyed proofreader.

Special thanks to the formidable band of "Torkidlit" writers for keeping me up past my bedtime and lighting the spark that would become this book.

Many thanks to the Ontario Arts Council for supporting this project through the Writers' Reserve Program.

Much love and gratitude to Gordon and Shirley Pape for ... well, everything.

Hugs to my sweet Jonah and Dahlia for so generously sharing

me with their character "siblings" and for inspiring me with their brilliant *joie-de-vivre*.

And finally, a universe of thanks to Jordy for being my best friend and putting up with my cranky writing moods all these years. If people were fonts, you'd be **bolded**, <u>underlined</u> and *italicized* on every millimetre of my heart. Always.